# QUEENIE & CO

GW00703335

*For Bill Brown*
*wherever he may be*

# QUEENIE & CO

## Francesca Jones

First published in Great Britain in 1993 by
Nexus
332 Ladbroke Grove
London W10 5AH

Typeset by TW Typesetting, Plymouth, Devon
Printed and bound in Great Britain by
Cox & Wyman Ltd, Reading, Berks

ISBN 0 35232 849 5

This book is a work of fiction.

In real life, make sure you practise safe sex.

# 1

## Once a Jolly Shagman

... I have recently struck up an intimate relationship with two most delightful young ladies. Intelligent, pretty, very sexy, highly talented, together they form a journalistic team which has become remarkably successful in the last two years.

Queenie is the writer. She is English, a willowy, sensuous natural redhead, a member of one of our many impoverished aristocratic families. Let me qualify that; by impoverished I suppose I mean struggling to keep up the image and traditions. A country mansion in Bedfordshire, the family seat, remains their home; at least, one small wing of it does, whilst the rest of the pile is open to the public, and there's a zoo in the garden. Queenie went through the usual upbringing of a girl of her class – you know the sort of thing: Roedean, Swiss finishing school, debutante et cetera. But she was well aware that there was barely any family cake left for her to cut a slice of, and that to enjoy a life of leisured luxury she was going to have to marry into it. Having no inclination for early domesticity shared with some chinless wonder or other, she opted for work. This could have meant running the family zoo but, as it happened, she was being humped at the time by the proprietor of the local rag, a friend of her daddy, the Duke of Granville, and by virtue of this fact she became a journalist. She very quickly acquired an excellent nose for the work; her reporting was smooth, concise and witty, and at the remarkably young age of twenty she found herself employed by a national tabloid.

Co is quite different – except in her needful sexual inclinations. Her full name is Coco Qua Min Baker, and she is the ravishing twenty-two year old offspring of a Filipino woman and an American GI, one of the uncountable results of relationships formed during the Vietnam war. Quite a bit shorter than Queenie, she has a cuddly, curvaceous body, long straight hair to the small of her back, shining as black as cracked-open pitch, and ebony eyes to match. She's the photographer. In America she was winning photographic competitions from age fifteen. By the time she reached twenty she was experienced in all branches of the art from glamour to action, and examples of her work had been published in magazines throughout the world.

Queenie and Coco were both twenty-one – only three months separate them – when chance flung them together and into each other's arms. An initial, tempestuous affair settled down into a loving, friendly relationship in which they spent much of their time living together, whilst respecting one another's need for constant variety in their AC/DC sex lives.

They became a team. Since both of them were well known and respected in the media world they found they were offered a choice of independent commissions for major publications. That's how we met. They did a piece on us, myself and my husband Lord Ballington, staying with us for a few days at our invitation – and sexually dallying with us, as you can imagine.

The more they told me, at that time, about their most recent, completed commission, the more it fascinated me. What they had produced for *Madame* was a wonderful story about the lives of gamblers on and off a junket cruise on a two-week trip out of Hong Kong and into the South China Sea, stopping off at Taiwan and the Philippines. However, what they related to me was quite another story. It was worthy, I began to realise as it unfolded, of novelisation. During the course of what was planned to be a simple journalistic job, they had managed to get themselves enmeshed in a frightening web of intrigue and deadly danger, not to mention extraordinary sexual adventures. My God, I thought that I, Frannie, had enjoyed libidinous experiences to cap just about all, but these two wanton, delicious creatures actually seemed to have matched me!

What made the prospect of writing a book about them exciting, as those bawdy days with them at Stratton Castle reached their end, together with the junket story, was the wealth of material I would have to work with. When she had not been tape-recording interviews, Queenie had taken detailed notes of all that transpired, where and how, sex a major part of it, and Coco's photos were by no means restricted to the scenery and gamblers at the tables. Coco, let me tell you, would be worth her weight in gold to a porn magazine!

Enough. Let's on with the story. I'll begin – why not? – with sex.

The pink, frothy pile of bubbles heaved upwards and Queenie Granville's head, her copper-red hair covered in foam, burst through them. Opening the palest of green eyes, Queenie blinked away the foam flecks and glanced through her bathside picture window; below her the lights from thousands of boats in Victoria Harbour were twinkling in the gathering Kowloon dusk, backdropped by Hong Kong Island itself with its frenetic collection of waterfront buildings. She smile contentedly, cracking a pretty dimple high up on her left cheek; it was great to be finally away from London and in this exotic place, relaxing in the super-luxury Regent Hotel before the start of a promising new assignment.

Sitting up, she brushed soapy pink fluff from her firm, freckly breasts, smoothing them and luxuriating in the touch of her slippery hands. She was not particularly vain – otherwise she would most certainly have insisted on the use of her courtesy title of Lady Queenie Granville – but she was acutely aware of her body, proud of her curvy height and long legs, ever content to pamper herself, and especially happy to indulge in delights sexual.

'Co?' she called out, glancing across the sybaritic, pale blue, Italian-marble bathroom towards the half-open door. She repeated herself louder in order to defeat the voice of Dinah Washington which drifted across the bedroom from the sitting-room. 'Coco!'

Barefoot, her stubby little toes painted emerald green, Coco Qua Min Baker padded into the bathroom, glossy, straight black hair swaying over white-laced shoulders, designer-jean-encased hips snaking. 'Betcha I know what you want,' she said, her accent faintly American.

'Right.' With a grin, Queenie bent forward until her nipples were in foam, ducking her head and pulling her hair forward with one hand to offer her back and swannish neck.

Coco picked up a sponge and dipped it in the bathwater, then soaped it, before squeezing it over her girlfriend's neck to bring a shudder of pleasure to those hunched shoulders. 'How do you feel? Excited?' she asked, as she ran the sponge down over the knobs of Queenie's spine.

'I'll say. He's such a scrumptious hunk of a man.'

'I didn't mean about him, screwball. I was referring to tomorrow, the start of the trip.' Coco's black eyes were shining as she plunged the sponge below the water in the swell of Queenie's buttocks, lingered there, then slid it up her back again.

'Tomorrow? Well, naturally. But I was rather more dwelling on the, ah, potential of friend Jamie Bond.'

'We'll find out soon enough, I guess – unless we've scared him half to death, the two of us inviting him up here alone for dinner.'

'Scared? I doubt that, darling. Seems to me he's the typical macho Australian. He's got to have balls to be the owner of a gambling ship. What's more, he's so young to have got where he has. He can't be older than thirty.' She wriggled contentedly. 'Keep doing that. It's heaven.'

'And a name to match. Jamie Bond!'

4

'We're going to have fun with him, I feel it, you know what I mean?'

'You can be such a randy bitch!'

'Can I not.' Queenie straightened up, letting her lank, wet hair drop over her shoulders. Her eyes moved softly over those of her friend's, and her dimple cracked. 'Do my tits?'

'You bet.'

'Fung Shui,' said Jamie Bond, an hour later, through a succulent mouthful of fried shrimp with tangerine jam. 'It's a superstition which abounds in the islands. People live their entire lives around it. It has a lot to do with physical harmony between nature and the elements. For instance,' he stared out through the huge floor-to-ceiling window which continued through the floor above, 'the island's main dragon is said to live up there on the peak behind the harbour; therefore it's the territory's most auspicious residential area, ergo the prices match it.'

Queenie studied him over the top of a glass of the fiery, warmed shao-shing wine. Apart from anything else, she was impressed with his size; he was six feet three with matching shoulders shown to advantage beneath his cream dinner jacket. He was clean-shaven, with a big, square, rugged face which she somewhat doubted denoted the frank honesty which it purported.

'I heard that a whole lot of apartments have fish tanks or mirrors just inside the front doors, to ward off evil spirits?' she said.

'Fung Shui again. You find it everywhere. Not everyone believes it, but I'd say the majority do.'

' "Superstition is the religion of feeble minds." Edmund Burke,' quoted Queenie. She smugly sipped her wine.

'Come again?'

'Uh-oh. She's off.' Coco smiled, a forkful of freshwater eel in broadbean sauce hovering near her mouth. 'Frightful intellectual, you know,' she said, in a fair imitation of Queenie's British upper-class accent. 'Classical education and all that kind of stuff. Can't resist the chance to show it off.' She slipped the eel between the full, scarlet-painted lips.

'My only vice,' Queenie responded.

'Hah!'

Jamie eyed her speculatively, his gaze briefly dwelling on the décolletage of her peach, antique-lace dress before sliding his eyes up to her face. 'You don't look like an intellectual,' he commented. 'I understood they were dowdy and wore bi-focals.'

'Coco was teasing. I'm not an intellectual.'

'And she doesn't wear bi-focals – but she is bi!' Coco wickedly slipped in.

Jamie's mouth fell slack as he stared in mild, amused astonishment from one gorgeous young lady to the other. 'I take it you do mean . . .?'

'Bi-sexual, yes,' Coco finished for him.

Laughing inwardly because this was not the first time Coco had employed a similar ruse for getting the subject around to sex, Queenie feigned indignation. 'Really Co,' she complained, 'that's absolutely a private matter. Apart from which you'll embarrass our guest.'

'Embarrass?' protested Jamie, 'What, me? Hell no. I'm an Aussie, remember? We don't get embarrassed!'

'Ah.' Coco drained her wine, watching him with keen interest. The personal butler who was part of the famed hotel's service stepped from where he had been hovering unobtrusively in a corner, and refilled the glass. 'You are aware, then, why we asked you to dinner, Mister 007?'

'To chat me up about the coming junket, I guess. To smooth the way with me so as to be sure you'll have maximum access to passengers and crew.'

'Well, how about that?' asked Queenie.

'You've got it, sister. As much freedom as you want. Jeez, an article in *Madame's* just terrific payment.'

Coco forked the final morsel of the delicious eel into her mouth, contriving to let Jamie catch a glimpse of it on the tip of her tongue as the butler whisked her plate away.

'I'll need to get in-depth interviews with as many passengers as are willing,' said Queenie. 'And Coco will

6

take hundreds, if not thousands, of photographs. She always does on an assignment like this.'

'That's fine with me. Two lovely sheilas like you aren't likely to upset many people. But one or two, you might. I'd better warn you, we get some fairly oddball characters aboard. They're a bunch of heavy gamblers; in lots of cases their bread comes from Christ knows where. They're not all going to submit to being third-degreed. Just use your loaves, and I doubt if you'll get into too much aggro.'

Later – the butler dismissed, the table cleared – as the three of them relaxed with coffee and liqueurs, Coco, a bit heady from the wine, said, 'So why did we ask you to dinner, Jamie?' She was sprawled in a big, comfortable, brocaded armchair facing him, with the hem of her green satin dress above her crossed knees, offering him a view of the back of one thigh almost up to her flesh-coloured stocking tops.

He frowned, not failing to notice the legs. 'I thought we'd just been into all that. You have *carte blanche*, like I said.'

Queenie was perched next to him on a sofa. Carefully, she put her glass down on a side table. She turned to face him, dropping a hand lightly on his knee.

'Actually,' she said slowly, 'what Co means is that that wasn't quite the only reason for our invitation.'

'Wasn't it?' he responded with an outer calmness which, within him, was rapidly dissolving. His greyish eyes hovered on hers, then shifted to the provocative hand.

'Guess?'

'I wouldn't dare, lady.'

'We've, ah, we've rather got the hots for you!'

His Adam's apple jiggled as his lips formed a soundless, 'Oh'.

'Well, since Aussies don't get embarrassed . . .' Queenie leant towards him, planting a little kiss on his cheek and reaching to undo his bow-tie. 'Why don't I get you nice and comfortable?'

'I'll rearrange the atmosphere,' said Coco, brightly. Getting up, she turned on the piped music and lowered the lights with a dimmer switch.

Jamie sank back into the sofa as Queenie made short work of his tie. 'Jesus, if I were a chick and you were two guys, I'd probably be hollering rape by now,' he said.

'Don't you believe it,' Queenie muttered, unbuttoning his shirt. 'Well, I certainly wouldn't – that is, not if the two guys looked anything like you. I wouldn't!'

'Me neither!' trilled Coco as she moved in on the other side of him. In the background Carmen McRae was singing 'Imagination'.

'You two always come on like this?' Jamie's eyes followed Queenie's hand with its long, silver-painted fingertips as it slid inside his opened shirt and through the mat of brown hair on his chest.

She snuggled up to him, rubbing her cheek on the bared chest, while the hand slid down to his belly where it encountered nothing but hairy-skinned muscle. 'On the occasional, special occasion.'

'You wouldn't want to crease up your smart jacket, would you?' asked Coco.

'Lean forward a bit.'

He grinned. 'It seems I'm in your capable hands.' He rocked slightly at the waist and she eased the jacket off him, managing to turn the sleeves inside out in the process.

'That's better.' Coco's eyes roved over Queenie, who had hooked a knee over Jamie's thigh and was snuggling even closer. Her skirt had ridden up to expose black stocking tops. 'Well, just so long as she's nice and comfy.' She put the flat of her hand on his opposite cheek and turned his face towards hers. Finding his lips, she kissed them with an eager tenderness which, at first, despite what was happening to him, caught him off guard, and then added to his growing arousal as her tongue insisted its way inside his mouth.

As the kiss lingered on, Queenie got busy pulling his shirt from his trousers. Then her hand strayed to her friend, and clutched a breast as if she were testing a melon for firmness.

Jamie Bond, proud, sometimes boastful, veteran of countless sexual adventures, had never found himself in such an extraordinary, delicious situation. He had made love with two girls together on several occasions, but only when he had been the instigator, or paying for it in oriental brothels. But this was surely something else. Not only were they making all the moves, but here were two of the loveliest chicks he had ever been alone with. Astonishment waning, erection rising, barely able to believe his luck, he let himself be rushed along with the flow.

Coco's mouth remained enmeshed with Jamie's. Queenie's hand rummaged inside the unzipped top of her girlfriend's dress as her passion – invariably needing only the minimum of encouragement – rose. Her free hand found Jamie's heavy thigh, and crept up it until it quickly achieved its libidinous objective. Grunting into Coco's mouth, Jamie spread his legs and heaved his hips. The heady combination of lips, tongue, hands and draping, bared thighs – plus the sight of one of Coco's breasts freed from her dress and wrapped in Queenie's squeezing hand – brought him to full, straining hard-on.

'My, my,' muttered Queenie, smirking, as she did much the same to Jamie's cock through his trousers as she was already doing to Coco's tit. 'I see you really like us, then!'

Coco freed her mouth from his. 'Let me feel that,' she insisted. As her hand replaced Queenie's on his hard-on, she exclaimed, 'Wow! You're big, aren't you?' Suddenly she was sliding from the sofa, pulling Jamie's thighs wide apart and dropping on her knees between them, the top of Queenie's thigh pressing into the side of hers. 'Let's take a look at that thing,' she murmured. 'Unzip him, Queenie love.'

Queenie, her head lying flat amongst the hairs of Jamie's chest, a lustful smile on her face, did the job with nimble precision. First the belt. Then two little buttons holding the trouser top. Her silver thumbnail uppermost on the zipper, index finger beneath it, with the controlled, practised smoothness of hundreds of such encounters with a man's trousers, she slid it all the way down as his breath caught in his throat. Immediately, Coco's impatient fingers took

9

a dive under the top of his white briefs, found their prize and hauled it into view, as Queenie's hand pulled down the front of the briefs and hooked them under his bulging testicles.

'Oooo!' breathed Queenie, impressed. 'I'll say he's big God!'

Eight and three-quarter inches, to be precise, and five and a half around. He had tape measured it on a number of occasions; it never varied. Jamie Bond was justifiably proud of his equipment, and having it brought into the air in this fashion by two beautiful, ultra-horny young ladies was blowing his mind.

Coco, licking her lips, her face wearing the habitual expression of wonder it did whenever she discovered a new penis, began to slowly masturbate him as he reached for and fondled her one exposed breast. As he hoped and anticipated, her mouth opened and her head ducked as she sheathed her lips over his cock, black eyes narrowing on his as she did so.

This was one of many acts sexual in which Coco – known since age sixteen as the hottest of stuff – revelled, and she went to it with great gusto, her tongue busily flicking on the underside of Jamie's cock as she slid her mouth over it, one hand cupping his balls. Queenie, her knickers dampening as she watched, and her pulse quickening, hoarsely muttered, 'Lift your backside a bit.'

He complied and, with her leg still hooked over his, she took hold of the top of his trousers and underpants and hauled them together down his sturdy, strong thighs until they were obstructed by her leg.

Unmouthing him and laying a hand over his on her breast, her eyes sliding from his face and down his torso to rest on his hard-on, Coco said, 'Are you a stayer, 007?'

'Yeah,' he drawled. 'If you don't drive me too flaming mad!'

'Like to see us undress each other?'

'Nah!'

'You first, then – you look indecent like that!' Quickly, Coco pulled off his shoes and socks. She pushed Queenie's thigh off his and, on her knees still, stripped off his trousers and pants, leaving them in a heap on the carpet.

Briefly, she sank back on her haunches, eyeing his unflagging erection, her tongue wetting her lips. Her head cocked to one side, she said, 'Play with yourself if you like. We shan't mind.'

'We'd like that,' confirmed Queenie. She slid to the carpet. 'C'mere,' she said, crooking her finger at her girlfriend. On her knees, Coco moved towards Queenie. As Carmen McRae warbled 'Sunshine of My Life', facing one another they stripped each other's dresses to their waists. Neither wore a bra, and the nipples of their full, firm breasts were erect.

Jamie failed to masturbate, but his eyes lustfully drank in every move, his mind indelibly committing this scene to memory as it was enacted before him. Coco, mouth clamped over Queenie's nipple, pulled the zip at the back of the antique-lace dress down as far as it would go, eased the dress over her hips and into a pile at her knees, then lowered black silk panties over sheer black stockings to join it.

Queenie, three-quarters facing the mesmerised Jamie, was fully sexually exposed to him; he dragged in a sharp little breath at the sight of her lush, coppery bush, red as her hair, provocatively framed by a black suspender belt and the whitest of white thighs and belly.

Two of Queenie's fingers found their way between her own legs, but were straight away removed and replaced by two of Coco's. Coco slid them up her friend's wet, tight little hole, saying, 'I'll do that. You do me.'

Moments later, Coco was in a similar state of *déshabillé* as Queenie. They closed lecherously into each other amidst their piles of clothing. Queenie's fingers found Coco's pussy, her other hand raided her buttocks, as bodies and mouths clashed steamily.

'Fuck me!' muttered Jamie, fighting to keep himself under control as the two girls did to one another what he was tempted to do to himself. 'I don't fucking believe this!'

Coco heard him. Breaking off her embrace to a grumbled complaint from Queenie, she stood up and stepped out of her clothing. Facing Jamie, she kicked off her high heels. Her heavy black bush was as straight as her hair; a thin line of pubic hairs ran tantalisingly upwards to her navel. On her flat little belly, to one side of her pussy, was a diamond-shaped mole; at the top of the inside of the opposite thigh was a tiny, tattooed, red rose.

'You'd better believe this!' she murmured, climbing on to the sofa, straddling his thighs, taking him in hand, positioning him and sinking down on to his penis – all the way until he was buried in her to the hilt, their pubic hairs intermingling.

As she impaled herself she bit her bottom lip, her eyes closed, her nostrils flared and she grunted heavily.

Meanwhile Queenie, kneeling on the carpet, her fingers inside herself once more, ogled this penetration from the rear and moaned, 'Bloody greedy bitch!'

The music changes, though not its mood, as Frank Sinatra sings 'My Funny Valentine', and Coco, making all the action, fucks Jamie to a love song, jiggling contentedly up and down on him, tits bouncing, hands gripping his shoulders. Queenie, greedy for a close-up, sinks again to her knees, this time between Jamie's splayed thighs and, panting a little as she masturbates, reaches out her free hand to explore Jamie's jiggling scrotum.

007 Jamie remains happy, vastly happy to let the ladies dictate the action. A state of euphoria, undoubtedly helped along by the Chinese wine, has descended on him; he had entered a fantasy land where few men actually get to tread. Though not far from orgasm, he is close enough to be savouring the near-ecstasy of pre-orgasmic pleasure, is contained enough to hover there.

Coco is not, however. She is one of those girls who come a lot – more so, in one session, than Queenie – and now she produces a final, vigorous, ball-breaking bounce, her breasts flying, squeaks her pleasure through closed lips, and is still, head drooping, eyes closed, hands steepling together over her very wet pussy.

Slowly, Coco topples sideways on to the sofa, luxuriating in her inner fire which is but slightly quenched.

Jamie murmurs, 'Yeah!' as Queenie, eager for a taste of Coco's juices on his cock, closes her lips over it. She is ravenous, this lovely redhead with the freckled tits. After a short session of her frenziedly sucking and wanking him, he is obliged to push her face away. 'I'll come in your mouth!' he gasps.

'No. Maybe later,' she breaths. 'Fuck me? Please? Like this?' She moves to one side of him, still on her knees, flattening her forearms and cheek on the sofa, and, for the first time since the sex began, Jamie moves from his sprawled-back position, kneels behind her and thrusts himself all the way into her until his balls meet the back of her long, milky thighs.

'Ow!' she goes. 'Yes, yes. I like that. Bang it into me. Bang that monster dick up my cunt!' and her dirt-talk does even more for him than the fact of breaching his second pussy within fifteen minutes. He slams it into her, the urge to come sweeping over him as strongly as it had done with his cock in her mouth. So he stops very still, fighting this until the need subsides, then he heaves into her again, and her dangling tits tremble.

Coco's lovely black eyes don't stay long shut with all this going on. They open wide and feast greedily on the naked rutting, and her pussy is once again seized with an overwhelming need. There is just room, on the big sofa, for her to ease her body between Queenie's head and the sofa's back, where she sits with legs apart, drawing her bare feet up to touch each other on Queenie's back. Swivelling her head, Queenie is confronted, not six inches away, with her girlfriend's big, black bush, the lips of her pussy held slightly, invitingly apart by emerald-nailed fingertips. Coco bumps her buttocks forwards, Queenie's tongue darts into the sweet, familiar-tasting vagina, her hands slide behind Coco's buttocks and she is in bi-sexual heaven as Jamie humps her and she eats her girlfriend in a rhythm complementary to his pounding.

Jamie, presented with this new diversion, is under-

13

standably losing control. Trying very hard to regain it, he stills within Queenie, but watching her slurping away between Coco's legs while her pussy throbs on him is now too much for him. 'I'm going to come,' he grunts. 'I'm going to come!' Abandoning all attempt at control, he slams into Queenie so hard that the slap of his thighs against her buttocks echoes through the big room. He holds for a second, then slams into her again.

Coco, eyes gleaming, keeping her pussy clamped against Queenie's mouth, grabs her buttocks and leans as far forward as she can, urging, 'Give it to me. Give it to me!' Her mouth opens wide, her tongue flattening below it, its tip curling like a beckoning finger, her eyes leching in the region of Jamie's belly as, quite, quite sure what this amazing chick is after, and his climax rushing over him, he uncouples from Queenie, grabs his cock, points it at the waiting face and erupts with a massive grunt. His sperm shoots across a foot and a half of space, hits Coco high up on one cheek, splashes down across it, over her lolling tongue and into her mouth, then her hair and across one shoulder; his second and third, less impressive, ejaculations drip over Queenie's back and buttocks.

Coco sighs another orgasm. Her face gleaming with semen, she swallows down the drops which her mouth has been savouring, then straightens and mutters to a sagging Jamie, 'I hope there's more – for later?'

'I'm bushed,' he groans, and he slowly heels sideways. His wilting penis shiny with Queenie's juices, he collapses on the carpet.

A song and a half later, Coco was at the mini-bar, fixing a whisky for Jamie, then opening for herself a baby champagne, her favourite tipple, whose brand did not matter that much to her as long as it bubbled. As Jamie hauled himself from carpet to sofa, parking his bare behind next to Queenie, who lay curled up, hugging her knees, Coco brought him his drink and handed it to him with the words, 'Lead in your pencil.'

Smiling crookedly, he knocked back the erstwhile contents of a miniature Chivas Regal bottle in two quick draughts, and held out the glass for more. 'With you two sex maniacs it looks like I'm gonna need it!' he said. 'Another?'

'Just so long as it doesn't give you brewer's droop.'

His eyes clamped randily on Coco's delectable buttocks as she snaked back to the bar, he muttered, 'Unlikely, kid. Unlikely.'

Lazily, Queenie reached a hand for him. Taking hold of his flaccid penis she gently squeezed it. 'What do you call our friend?' she asked.

'Call it? Are you nuts?'

'I had a boyfriend once who called his Tarzan. He wasn't nuts.'

'And I suppose he called your pussy Jane.' He took his fresh drink from Coco. 'What did you do – swing on it?'

Coco laughed. 'Oh, she swung on it all right!'

Tugging Jamie's penis as if pulling a bell-rope, Queenie said, 'We'll call this Arnold – after that Schwarzenegger hunk.'

'You're both bananas!'

'And Arnold's a cucumber.' Queenie could feel stirrings inside her fist. 'An inflatable cucumber.'

'Certainly not the vicarage tea-party variety,' said Coco. She sat down on the arm of the sofa, watching Queenie's manual ministrations, while sipping her champagne. Despite her orgasms, or maybe because of them, she felt hornier than ever. Her free hand dropped between her legs, a finger penetrated. 'Get it up, Queenie,' she breathed. 'Get that big thing right up again.'

'Arnold,' said Queenie. 'All solid muscle.'

'I don't believe you two!'

'We're going to have you jumping like a kangaroo, Mister Australia.' Queenie fisted the speedily growing cock harder and faster.

'Picture time.' Putting down her half-full glass, Coco went to a wardrobe. From it she produced a Polaroid camera.

'What the hell?' grunted Jamie as she pointed the lens at him and Queenie.

'Just a wedding photo, or two. For our album.'

'Hey! No you don't!' Jamie protested, as the flash momentarily blinded him.

'Ooops, sorry!' exclaimed Coco as, with a tiny whirring noise, the blank picture slid out of the camera's front.

'You can turn that in, kid. I'm not into being a porn star,' Jamie objected.

'Come on, spoilsport. It's just a bit of fun. I'll burn them later if you care that much.' Coco waved the picture in the air as the print began to appear. 'Don't tell me you've never done this before?'

'I've taken shots of a few sheilas minus their gear, sure.'

'There you are, then. So now one's shooting you.'

'I bet Arnold won't object. He's very proud of himself,' said Queenie, at last letting go of Jamie's penis, which stood stiffly pointing at the ceiling. 'He's ready already!'

Coco appraised the clean, damp print. 'Let's call this an engagement picture.' She padded back to the sofa, handing the print to Jamie. 'Don't smudge it.'

'Why? I thought you were going to destroy it later?' But he took it carefully between finger and thumb.

'Not it. Them. Only if you absolutely insist.'

'Christ.' He gaped at the snap of himself and Queenie. It seemed that she had swung one thigh well apart from the other just for the benefit of the camera, since, next to him now, her knees were back together. His penis was poking up through her fist, her eyes drooped sulkily while his looked shocked, and her coppery pussy was on clear show between the parted, black-stockinged legs. The picture was very clear, even to the freckles on her breasts.

'Not bad, huh?' opined Coco.

'Very bad. Very, very bad.' He handed it back to her and she laid it face-up on an occasional table.

'Now for some honeymoon shots. Get down to it, you two swinging young lovers.'

Queenie, aching now for further penetration, Queenie who had yet to climax, positioned herself on her back on the sofa, her knees spread, and very high because she was

16

still wearing high-heeled shoes; their tips dug into the outside of Jamie's thigh. Opening her arms, she beckoned him. 'Roll over and fuck me, 007?'

His weight was on his arms and he was lowering himself on top of her, her hand guiding his penis to her vagina, when Coco fired another shot. Ignoring the flash he slid 'Arnold' deep within her, rocking smoothly as her feet rose over the small of his back, till her knees almost touched her shoulders.

Coco moved behind to take another picture. She shot the entire pack of eight in quick succession, not even pausing between them for the prints to develop, but dropping each one face-up on the table as Jamie's screwing speeded up and Queenie's moans became more urgent. Then she slotted in a new pack and moved closer. Dropping to one knee near Queenie's head, and holding the camera in one hand while the fingers of the other played with Queenie's stiff nipple, Jamie still pounding away, she muttered, 'Are you coming, now, honey?'

Queenie's moan became a grunt, then she produced a strangled 'Oh, yeeeees!' Letting go of the nipple, Coco focused the camera on her face. Queenie's eyes closed tight, her head tilted back into the unruly bunches of red hair. Her mouth sagged wide in a silent scream as her face contorted in an ecstatic grimace, she shook her head as if in a violent 'no', and climaxed with a rushing sigh as Coco took two more pictures.

With Jamie continuing to heave away, Queenie's features relaxed into their habitual, lovely serenity, her mouth closed and her eyes too. Coco laid pictures and camera on the carpet, well clear of the scene of action, then lowered her lips next to Jamie's ear and dropped a hand on his heaving buttocks.

'Hold it, buster,' she muttered. 'Ease up. The lady's in heaven – and me, I'm in hell. I need you!'

He turned to look at her, his forehead beaded with perspiration. Amusement lustfully crept into his unglazing eyes as his bottom stilled. 'Any way you like it, sister.'

'You a back-door man, man?' she asked.

He rolled off Queenie, who remained comatose, her breasts gently heaving. 'Nothing queer about me, baby.'

'For sure. But how about fucking me like a bitch on heat? A dirty bitch. From behind.'

His eyes narrowed. She could almost see his pulse accelerating, 'Try me.'

Her eyes fell on a comfortable armchair. 'There, no?'

'Doggy time,' he commented, standing up and holding his penis as he followed her. As she knelt in the armchair, her forearms resting along its back, hands overlapping, her chin propped on the backs of her fingers, he murmured, 'Better change its name from Arnold to Rover!'

She wriggled her bottom dissolutely as he eased two fingers into her vagina. Queenie's eyes came open, instantly feasting; the Moody Blues played 'Isn't Life Strange'. Needing to bend slightly at the knees, she wrapped a hand around the front of her thigh and fisted his glans to her waiting hole.

'Ready?'

'Yes, please,' sighed Coco. She gasped as his gorged penis began to stretch her. 'Good dog!'

'Rrruufff!' Jamie growled.

Relentlessly, fraction by fraction, Jamie's powerful penis slides into Coco. Her eyes close. She bites the skin of a knuckle soundlessly, keeping her body very still, managing not to sag forward. Her vaginal walls give, relax and, in the instant, Coco is in ecstasy, Jamie's fine cock arousing her G-spot as he crams it slowly all the way up her, filling her in the very special, wonderfully dirty way that a doggie-fuck does, and she gasps, 'Oh, yeah, yeah, yeah, yeaaaah.' Further aroused by the sound of her voice, her choice of words, she mutters, 'Bang it in me, you filthy bastard. Bastard!'

Jamie finds a rhythm. That tight little pussy and her extraordinary excitement contrive to bring him to a magnificent high as his eyes lech on the sight of his cock poling steadily, slowly, beneath as shapely a pair of buttocks as he has ever encountered.

He blinks as the flash goes off again. Queenie now, with

the Polaroid – re-aroused by Coco's treatment, takes pictures, circling the rutting pair, shooting, laying a picture face up, shooting again, another angle, then two more. When there is only one left, she strings the camera around her neck, perches on the arm of the sofa and ogles the copulation, masturbating, eyelids sagging.

Coco also performs the onanistic sin. Her entire body trembles with the delirium of a fast-approaching orgasm, her fingers move faster on her clitoris as Jamie, himself climbing orgiastic mountains, bangs it into her, balls jumping forward with every determined thrust, in time with the jiggle of Coco's tits. No silent climax for Coco this time; she screams into the backs of her hands.

Grabbing the camera with both hands, her voice shaking with excitement, Queenie says loudly, urgently, as if she is his sexual partner, 'Are you coming, Jamie? Are you coming?' And, as he nods vigorously, his teeth bared, she grabs his hip with one hand and drags him backwards, grating the words, 'Over her, come over her.' As Jamie's penis slides out of Coco, Queenie grasps the camera with two hands and aims.

Jamie erupts while Coco sinks into the chair, her nose sliding down its back. Sperm arches, splashing over her knobby spine and white buttocks, as Queenie fires off the camera's final shot. He is still ejaculating, grunting with each diminishing spurt, as Queenie, camera dangling, straps indenting her nipples, jams two fingers of one hand up her vagina and with two of the other hand furiously rubs her clitoris, coming along with Jamie to a loud sigh of contentment, joyous to have achieved one of those rare occasions when she climaxes more than once in so short a period.

Sex, on this libidinous evening, reigns supreme!

Reanimation took a little while. Then it was Jamie who fixed the drinks. Thumbing off the top of a baby champagne for Coco, which came free with a disappointing plop and no foam, he said, 'I just realised that none of us smokes.'

Coco fixed a contemplative gaze on his swaying penis as he crossed the room to her. 'No vices, that's us.'

'Sure.' Standing in front of her, while her eyes lingered on the same part of his anatomy, he filled a tulip glass with the champagne. Handing it to her, he murmured, 'None at all?'

'Very occasionally I smoke a cigar.' She dragged her eyes to the glass. 'Ta.'

'Very, very occasionally. She has a cock in her mouth more often than she does a cigar!' said Queenie mischievously.

Shaking his head in bemusement, Jamie returned to the minibar to mix himself a scotch and soda. 'Do all upper-class British journalists talk like that?' he asked.

Queenie smiled sweetly at his hefty buttocks. 'Only the female ones!'

He emptied the last of the miniature scotches into his glass. 'What would you like?'

'Whisky?'

'It's finished.' He glanced around the room. The three of them, except for Queenie's suspenders, shoes and stockings, were naked, their clothes strewn untidily all over the place. 'We can hardly call room service.'

'Why ever not?' asked Queenie innocently.

'Come on!'

'Just teasing. I'll settle for a beer.' She kicked off her shoes as he poured it and brought it over to her. 'My feet are killing me!'

The atmosphere remained charged with sexual electricity, though individual needs were no longer pressing and the three were comfortably relaxed in their nakedness. Coco gathered up the Polaroid snaps from table tops and carpet. She went through them slowly and pruriently, sitting beside Jamie on the sofa while Queenie, San Miguel beer in hand, leaned over its back.

'What a simply great shot of your face,' she commented, admiring one of the two close-ups of Queenie.

'I seem to be in mortal agony.'

'Ecstatic, you were. Not much difference between agony

and ecstasy, is there?' She paused. 'You were coming!'

Jamie grinned. 'I guess I did that to her.'

'Indeed you did. And you did this to me.' Coco being doggy-fucked, Jamie fully penetrating from behind, his head flung back, his neck sinews standing out. 'And this.' Jamie ejaculating over her back and buttocks.

Looking at the pictures brought a new stirring to Jamie's loins. 'Listen, ah, you don't have to burn them,' he decided. 'Provided you can let me have a couple.'

'I'll make you a copy of the whole set, if you like.' Coco stared at another shot, a pleased, lecherous expression on her face. 'Oooo, isn't that ever so nice!' Jamie enthusiastically giving it to Queenie.

'How are you gonna get copies? They're one-offs, no negs. You can hardly send them to Kodak,' Jamie observed.

'I'll photograph them and develop the negatives myself. I carry a kit with me, including a canvas darkroom. I always do my own developing when there's time.' She paused. 'Want them enlarged?'

'Hell, no.'

She glanced at his growing penis. 'Want that enlarged?'

'Hell, yes!'

'That's funny. So do I.' Slipping to her knees on the carpet, Coco opened her mouth and tongued his cock into it.

Leaning further over the back of the sofa for a closer look, Queenie raised an eyebrow, finishing off her beer without taking her eyes from Coco's fellation which quickly brought Jamie to full erection. 'Here we go again!' she happily observed.

# 2

# On Rupert, Bare

The square mile or so of placid water known as Victoria Harbour, which from the Regent Hotel at night presented itself as a mysterious, romantic stretch of near-black velvet, its edges shimmering with thousands of pinpricks of light, by day resembled some watery rubbish-dump.

At five o'clock in the afternoon of the following day, Jamie Bond's gambling cruise ship, the *Star of Kowloon*, Jamie on the bridge with his captain, nosed its way through a city of boats and a bog of flotsam and jetsam featuring, above all, discarded plastic bags.

A threatened typhoon had failed to materialise, the September sunshine was bearably hot, the humidity fractionally short of sticky. On the upper deck, Queenie and Coco lolled over the ship's rail, fascinated by the extraordinary, motley collection of boats through which the *Star of Kowloon* made its slow, careful passage, many of them looking as if they had been stuck together from discarded bits and pieces half a century before.

From one of the notorious brothel boats a group of whores waved. Nearby, one of a pair of junks moored together, their sides protected with old car tyres and with sagging green canvas shelters covering three-quarters of their decks, rocked with a jerky, regular motion which had little to do with any swell caused by the passing gambling ship, and sent the dirty harbour water sloshing up its sides.

22

Queenie, not slow to interpret something like that, pointed with a laugh, 'Know what that reminds me of? Teenage years in parked cars at night, at a favourite courting place on the edge of a Bedfordshire wood. Windows all steamed up, cars rocking, springs creaking.'

Coco watched in amused interest; as they drew further away from the junk, its motion intensified. 'You telling me someone's at it in there?' She took a quick picture with her Nikon.

'Can't think what else, can you? They're not playing patience.'

The dipping and plunging junk passed out of sight behind the stern of the *Star of Kowloon* as she slowly turned to port. Below them, in the mass of junks moored against one another, a sort of floating shanty town, a man was having his hair cut. 'This is an extraordinary place,' commented Coco, shooting another picture. She wrinkled her button nose. 'Pity about the smell.'

'Effluvia. You get used to it, apparently.'

'Can't say I want to.' As she expertly changed lenses from telephoto to wide angle, Coco said, 'Wonderful surprise, the suite we've been given.'

'As thanks for last night, and for certain ulterior motives, shouldn't wonder. It was obviously empty in any case, so it cost him nothing to switch us from an ordinary cabin to a special suite.'

'Great guy. Hope we see more of him.'

'We've seen all there is!'

Later, as they passed Chai Wan on the east coast of Hong Kong Island, the ship beginning to head out towards the South China Sea and its north-north-east course for Tai Wan, three hundred miles distant, Queenie, her red hair flying in the mounting breeze, suggested they explore.

The casino, colourful and well-ordered, caught them by surprise. They'd been at sea barely half an hour, yet it was already busy. Apart from the usual international games, there were others Queenie was unfamiliar with. One in particular caught her attention. Several people, all men, were seated around a large, square, blue-baize-covered table in the centre of which lay a heap of small ivory counters the size of large shirt buttons. Bets were placed and a croupier inverted what looked like a silver sundae cup over the pile, cutting into it, and swivelling the cup around to leave the majority of counters on the outside. The cup was then moved well away from these, to one side, and remaining counters, some thirty or forty of them, were carefully divided into sets of four with a curved ivory stick which had four semi-circular notches for that purpose. When there were only three left, various muted noises from the players signified defeat or victory, and bets were settled.

'What on earth is it?' asked Queenie, intrigued with the game, and aware of the tension surrounding the table. Her gaze riveted on a huge-bellied Chinaman with a bald head who had in front of him a big stack of large, yellow, folded, Hong Kong thousand-dollar bills.

'Fan-tan,' said Coco. 'One of the simplest games in the world, as easy as that Aussie twos-up game with coins. Bets are placed on how many counters are left when they have been separated into fours. None, one, two or three.'

'That's it?'

'Yup.'

'Don't they get bored?'

'You kidding? Next to mah-jong it must be the biggest gambling game in China.' She looked around the table. 'Don't seem too friendly a lot, do they?'

'Hardly your family roulette game.' They were generally Asian faces, mainly Chinese, but also a couple at the table which could have been Australian or European. Not a single smile amongst them, they stared in grim concentration as the little Chinese croupier re-piled the counters and again worked the cup into the middle of the pile before pulling away the central section of it. Apart from the croupier, the table was still, holding its collective breath as he began to break down the remaining counters into sets of four at a time. The girls watched the pay-off, then wandered away past a line of blackjack tables and paused at a craps table where emotions were in lively contrast to those of the fan-tan game.

'Will you look at her!' exclaimed Queenie.

Waiting for a croupier to give the signal to throw, a pair of dice in her raised hand, looking as if preparing to hurl them clear across the casino, stood a tall, voluptuous, gorgeous blonde of about thirty, dressed almost entirely in expensive black leather: calf-length boots over black stockings, a mid-thigh skirt, just too long to be a mini, which clung sensuously to her well-defined haunches, a chrome-studded waistcoat and a fine white silk shirt with upturned collar. She had heavy but beautifully applied make-up accentuating Slavic cheekbones and a wide, full mouth.

As Coco found a slot at the table, Queenie peering over her shoulder, to the ritual words 'Shooter coming out. Let'em roll!' the woman flung the precision dice far more gently than her tensed arm suggested. They rattled fast down the table, bounced against a diamond-rubber studded end, and came to rest with a six and a one uppermost.

'Seven, a natural. Lucky seven,' called the croupier as the stick man raked in the dice and began to push piles of chips across the table towards the winners. The woman's slightly slanted, big green eyes danced with excitement as she let her winning pile of chips ride the 'Win' line.

Fascinated by her appearance, Coco was watching her closely, when she suddenly glanced up straight across the table and into her eyes. Green eyes locked for a few seconds on black ones; the woman's eyebrow curved upwards questioningly. Coco's tummy did a little nervous jump, then the woman looked down again, turning her attention to the dice which the stick man had pushed over to her.

'Did you catch that?' muttered Coco. 'The way she looked at me?'

'And the way you looked back. I did indeed, my pet. Lessy, I'd guess.'

'Put her on the top of your interview list.'

'You bet.'

They didn't play any tables, content to wander and to absorb the atmosphere. The gamblers were an extraordinary mixture, ranging from the archetypal wealthy middle-western American couple to the fiercest-looking Chinese who might have been from the echelons of one of the Triad secret societies.

As Queenie and Coco lingered at an American-style roulette table, where not a seat was to be had despite the house-percentage-doubling double zero, Jamie Bond suddenly appeared, keen to know how they liked his floating casino.

'Interesting,' said Queenie. 'By the way, many thanks for moving us to a suite.'

He cracked a grin. 'I would think it was the least I could do ... considering.'

Admiring the dashing figure he cut in an immaculate cream linen suit and navy silk cravat, and finding her sexual attraction to the man if anything stronger than ever, Queenie said, 'No doubt we can expect a social call in the near future?'

'That's, ah, on the cards, yeah.'

'Who's the big guy?' asked Coco, indicating a man even broader than Jamie himself. His bear-sized chest had a heavy gold chain resting on it, half buried in a mat of black hair beneath the open neck of a riotously coloured Haiwaian shirt. He was sitting near the spinning roulette wheel, tidying a heap of large-denomination chips in front of him. He had small watery-blue eyes in a pudgy, very white face, with a cleft chin and a cleft cheek to match. He looked unpleasant and very tough.

'Taciturn bastard,' said Jamie. 'Third time this year he's been on the trip. He's British, a Londoner. Max Masters, he calls himself. Big punter, so naturally I've had him at my table for dinner. He's one of those characters you've learnt next to nothing about after a two-hour conversation.' He paused. 'I doubt if he'll take kindly to being interviewed.'

As Jamie was speaking, the man looked up. Brushing a straying lock of brown hair from a forehead as crumpled as corrugated tin, he stared first at Queenie, then at Coco. His little eyes were expressionless, yet they managed, with swift up-and-down glances, to strip them both naked. Then, after dwelling briefly on Coco's breasts, which swelled temptingly under a tight white blouse, they swivelled back to the big roulette wheel, which rang with the tinkling of the bouncing ball.

Jamie grinned. 'What d'you know. He noticed you both!'

'All men are dirty bastards,' Coco commented.

'And aren't you just happy about it!' exclaimed Queenie.

'You two are nuts,' said Jamie. He nodded to the nearby fan-tan table. 'You see that fat, bald-headed Chinaman?'

'We noticed him, yes.' Queenie frowned. 'Sort of evil-looking.'

'He's been on this trip twice before, too. At the same time as Masters. They're kind of mates. His name's Li.'

'Strange bedfellows,' said Queenie.

'Villains, most probably.'

'They have girlfriends?'

'Masters came aboard this trip with a chick. I'd guess she's a Hong Kong whore.' He shrugged. 'Maybe they share her.'

'I bet there's a hell of a story floating around somewhere between the three of them,' said Coco.

'Let it float. In any case, Li's as close-mouthed as Masters. I wouldn't poke around there too much, if I were you. You're liable to walk straight into the shit.'

'Part of the job.'

'Yeah, well watch it. When do you start?'

'Tomorrow.'

'Take it in easy stages. Let people get to know you, and who you are – that you're harmless.'

'What do you think we're going to do?' Queenie objected. 'One thing we know is how to do our job.'

'Just warning you, that's all. Don't get touchy. Basically most of these people are no more than fanatic gamblers. But there are a few oddballs like Masters and Li. You never know, they could be dangerous. I wouldn't go popping off that camera at people without permission, Coco.'

'Usually, I don't. Not from close up, at least.' She paused, smiling artlessly. 'But I have ways and means when people say no.'

'I just bet you do.' Taking her hand he said, 'By the way, when do I get my prints?'

'Some day, your prince will come.' She laughed at her own joke. 'Have a little patience.' Her expression underwent a violent change as she grimaced, clutching her stomach. 'Suddenly I don't feel so well.'

'We are rolling a bit. You're not going to get sick, are you? I have the two of you planned for dinner with a partner of mine.'

'I'll take it easy for a bit, and lie down. I'll be okay.'

But okay Coco was not. She was overwhelmed by a violent attack of *mal de mer* which had her running between her bed and the bathroom, and convinced her she was about to die.

At nine o'clock Queenie, stunning in a black Balenciaga evening dress complemented by a single string of pearls, her hair swept high and with tear-shaped emerald earrings swinging at her sinuous walk, made her impressive entrance to the restaurant, alone.

Jamie Bond's companion was called Dominic Henry. He was tall and lean, dressed in an immaculately tailored white dinner-jacket with a maroon silk pocket handkerchief and matching, extravagantly flared bow-tie in a wing collar. He was about thirty, prematurely balding, thin black hair slicked straight back.

Queenie found herself attracted right away by him, particularly by his thin aristocratic nose and cynical, crooked smile.

'Par for the course for Coco would be until about lunchtime tomorrow,' said Jamie, as they sat down. 'What a pity.'

'I was looking forward to meeting her,' Dominic said, carefully adjusting a shirt cuff. His accent was very upper-class British. 'She can't surely be as beautiful as you?'

'Thank you.' Pleased, Queenie smiled. 'Coco's lovely.'

'Granville.' Dominic's wide-spaced, slightly drooping walnut eyes appraised her in frank admiration. 'Where are you from in England?'

'Bedfordshire.'

'Of course. Queenie Granville. I knew I'd heard the name. I've read some of your stuff. Enjoyable, as I recall. Your father's the Duke of Granville, right?'

'That's right.'

'Curious. He happens to be a friend of my dad's. The Marquess of Bream.'

'That would make you a lord. And me, I'm a lady. What do you know?'

'You bloody poms. What a load of piffle!' exclaimed Jamie.

'Agreed,' said Queenie. 'But it can be fun.'

'And useful on occasions, as you damn well know, Jamie. For instance, as chairman of this little enterprise why does my title appear gold embossed on the letterhead? Respectability – and you know it.'

Jamie spluttered. 'You're about as respectable as Ned Kelly!'

'Thanks. And this ship should be flying the Jolly Roger.'

'My, my.' Queenie frowned from one man to the other. 'You two wouldn't be getting into a fight, would you?'

A broad grin split Jamie's face in two. 'Hell, no – we never fight.' His heavy hand closed over the back of hers. 'So, it's Lady Granville, is it? Well, I'll be a . . .'

'Wrong, it's Lady Queenie,' Queenie interrupted. 'My father's a duke, do you see. I'm not married to a baron or anything – then I'd be a Lady whatever his surname was.'

'Beats me.' Looking her straight in the face with an expression bordering on a leer, he added, squeezing her hand, 'Some lady!'

Later, as they finished their satay – skewers of cooked, marinated meat kept warm on a brazier on the table, and complemented with side dishes of pungent peanut sauce – Queenie remarked, 'The food's excellent.' She glanced around the gently swaying restaurant, where only the

29

wine and water remained at a constant level. 'And it's nice that everyone's in black tie.'

'First and last night rule,' said Jamie. 'Rather like correct dress in casinos and Dominic's title on our letterhead. As he pointed out, it adds a veneer of respectability.'

'What friend Jamie is trying to say,' put in Dominic, 'is that when you get down to the nitty-gritty of the business, gambling is somewhat indecent. That is, casino gambling and organised trips like here on the *Star of Kowloon*. It attracts a doubtful element. Worse, perhaps, it leads decent people who get hooked on it to financial disaster, sometimes turning them into criminals to support the habit, even bringing about suicides.'

Jamie, who had been appreciatively sipping chilled Portuguese Vinho Verde as he listened, produced a satisfied smile. 'And it makes you and me buckets of lovely loot, old mate!'

'Exactly. Totally immoral!' Dominic's eyes were on Queenie's as he pronounced these words, and the way they burned into her brought a little thrill to her belly. She liked this man a lot. He had the air of a dissolute cavalier about him. She was finding the company of these two men, one of whom she had carnally enjoyed only the previous evening and the other with whom, her instincts told her, she was possibly going to have sex sooner or later, both stimulating and arousing.

Over coffee and a Tia Maria, Queenie, pleasantly light-headed, asked, 'Is it true that the Chinese will eat anything on four legs except the table?'

'I'll say. Boiled dogs, for instance,' said Jamie.

Queenie grimaced.

'You're unlikely to see it, but they tuck into such delicacies as monkey's brain, bear's paw and crane's gizzard,' Dominic added.

'Oh, come on.'

'I promise you. And they're damned expensive items, too.'

'Don't forget the snakes, Nick,' said Jamie, warming the bowl of a glass of Napoleon brandy between his palms.

Queenie shuddered. 'They eat snakes? I hate snakes!'

Dominic lit a cigar. 'It's not as expensive as the other treats. And I promise you it tastes quite okay. The more venomous the snake, the tastier. Supposed to have medicinal properties, too.'

'Load of balls,' opined Jamie, as his calf found Queenies below the table. 'Listen, I was going to suggest that the four of us went to my cabin for nightcaps. But since we're only three, I guess we'll go to the bar. A real live lady alone with a lord and a definite non-gentleman is not on, is it?'

Dominic said, 'It's okay. I'll leave you two alone.'

But Queenie, by now, was entertaining very different ideas. She was fast arriving at the stage where her libido ruled her head. She smiled from one man to the other with false demureness, feeling raunchily daring as she said to Dominic, the words catching in the back of her throat. 'You really don't have to do that, you know. Why don't we all three go and have a drink in Jamie's cabin?'

The pressure of Jamie's calf against hers increased. 'I dunno. We shouldn't, you know.'

'Try me.'

Rising, his lips silently forming the words 'we might' as he did so, and bringing a tingle to her spine, he put his hand on her elbow.

'Okay,' he said. 'Let's go.'

The master's suite was cheerfully opulent. The cabin below the lower front deck, just short of the prow of the boat, ran right across from port to starboard so that it had two pleasingly curved sides of highly polished, light wood planks with three gleaming brass portholes in each one. There was a beamed, wooden ceiling to match the sides, and more matching wood on the other two straight walls; and the deck was covered with a soft, cream fitted carpet, itself the host to several colourful rugs. Heavy, comfortable-looking cane furniture, liberally sprinkled with Indian silk cushions, was pleasingly arranged, and the lighting was from converted antique copper and brass oil lamps.

'Nice,' commented Queenie, as Jamie closed the door behind them. 'Very, very nice.'

'Does himself proud, the boss,' said Dominic.

The ship was rising and falling slowly through one to two feet from prow to stern, just enough for someone who had not quite got her sea-legs completely together to need to concentrate on balance, and Queenie staggered as she made her way to a chair.

'Pissed already?' said Jamie, from behind a curved cane bar where he was unscrewing the top off a Glenlivet malt whisky.

Queenie flopped awkwardly into the comfort of the chair, crossing her legs and hitching her dress up to her knees. As Jamie poured the malt over crackling ice-cubes in a cut-glass tumbler, more than half filling it, she said, 'I shall be if that's for me.'

'Nah. This is for me. Like some, too?'

'About half that measure.'

'It'll be more brandy for you, no, Nick?'

Dominic nodded. His droopy eyes fixed on Queenie's legs, he sank into a chair close by her. He must have felt her watching him watching her, because he said, 'Nice shoes,' before lifting his eyes to hers.

They were simple, black patent leather Gucci evening shoes with a tiny silver lamé bow on each of them. Queenie smiled at them, saying nothing as Jamie handed her a whisky.

'Mind if I put on some jazz?' asked Jamie. 'I'm a jazz freak.'

He had already downed half his drink, she noticed, but booze did not seem to have much effect on him.

'Whatever turns you on,' she said.

A half minute later the combined sounds of Sonny Rollins and Miles Davis, very soft, permeated the air from several strategically-placed speakers.

'Marvellous system,' commented Queenie.

'Only the best for the dear boy.' Dominic stubbed out his half-smoked cigar, his eyes still on Queenie as he sipped brandy from a glass which was a third again larger than his cradling, slim-fingered hand.

They chatted idly for a while, but more than their

instantly-to-be-forgotten conversation was on their minds. It was clear from the fractionally nervous way the men kept looking at her, and in her responses, that the promise of sex hovered in the air. The atmosphere was becoming charged with it; the sensuous, slow jazz seemed to add to it. Amazingly, since he had put away more than a bottle of wine with his meal and a huge brandy after it, Jamie quickly polished off his whisky. As he replenished the glass, he offered to show Queenie the rest of his suite – which, Queenie realised with a tremor of excited anticipation, meant the stateroom.

It was most extraordinary. Hard into the pointed nose of the ship, the bed was enormous, tailor-made to fit snugly there, a good eight feet wide at its bottom and tapering through another eight feet to its pointed top. It was half covered by a light-brown bearskin, the huge head of the bear intact and stuffed, its mouth gaping open to show a formidable set of teeth.

'Meet Rupert,' said Jamie.

'Rupert,' Queenie echoed blankly, blinking at the bearskin, swaying with her almost empty glass in hand. The prow of the boat made an unexpected dip causing her to stagger forward and slop the rest of her whisky on the deck.

Jamie grabbed her arm. Not content with simply stopping her from falling, and taking the long-awaited opportunity, he pulled her body tight into his and kissed her on the mouth.

'Perhaps it's time for me to say goodnight,' drawled Dominic. But he made no attempt to move from where he was leaning in the doorframe.

Jamie broke off the kiss. Keeping Queenie pulled close in to him, one hand curving over her buttock, he muttered while giving her bottom a suggestive squeeze, 'What do you say – shall he stay? I've noticed the looks you've been throwing his way.'

Queenie's insides gave a lurch which had nothing to do with the rocking of the boat. Now it seemed to be upon her, she was almost scared of this situation, hoping for it

33

though she had been. She swallowed, grinding her hips against Jamie, feeling a rising hard-on.

Dominic still leant in the doorway, watching them with a slightly twisted, unreadable smile. Slowly, she said, 'Why . . . doesn't . . . he . . . stay?'

'Close the door, mate,' Jamie exclaimed, almost breezily. 'Keep yourself on this side of it. Her ladyship here seems to be hankering after a bit of a threesome!'

There was a soft click, and the jazz became almost inaudible. With both Jamie's hands clutching her buttocks, Queenie watched over his shoulder as Dominic, taking his time, removed his jacket, folded it with studied care, and draped it over the back of a chair. 'Hit the lights, Nick . . .' Jamie muttered. 'Turn them way down low.'

The dimmer switches did their job as Queenie, a lump in her throat to match the size of Jamie's semi-erection, and abandoning herself to whatever was to happen, sought out Jamie's lips with her own. Dominic piled two cushions on the bed and stretched on it on his back next to the bearskin, hands behind his head on the cushions, eyes intent on the embracing couple. Jamie's buttock-groping fingers began to walk the material of Queenie's evening dress slowly up the back of her sheer-stockinged legs, crumpling it in a pile under his wrists until his hands fondled her bottom through fine white satin Christian Dior knickers.

Holding her lewdly like that, he turned them around so that her back was towards Dominic. 'Cast your peepers on this, mate . . .' he said. 'I'll bet money it's the finest piece of arse you've seen in a while.'

One hand kept Queenie's dress bunched above her hips while the thumb of the other hooked into the waistband of her panties and turned them inside-out down over her bottom, exposing its flesh to Dominic's plundering eyes, of which she was well aware even though she could not see them.

'Gorgeous!' The single word from the bed dripped with lust.

'Like that?' murmured Jamie in Queenie's ear, licking it

as the fingers of both hands hooked into her buttock flesh and rifled. 'Like your knickers down, don't you?'

'Mmmm.' Queenie wriggled against him, her hands linked behind his neck, waves of pleasure invading her.

'On the bed then. We'll get them off.' Letting the skirt fall, he walked her three backward paces to the edge of the bed, sat her on it near Dominic's feet, then, kneeling, reached under the dress, slid both hands up the outside of her legs, found her knickers and pulled them down and off over her shoes, while she watched him with big eyes, shoulders slumped, feeling wonderfully helpless. Grinning like a naughty schoolboy, he got up, crawled across the bed and stretched the knickers over the bear's head, so that an ear and half the side of its face stuck through each leg hole. 'Once upon a time,' he said, breaking momentarily the sexual spell, 'there were three bears. Mummy bear, daddy bear, and kinky bear . . .'

Queenie giggled, while Dominic produced the sort of guffaw which comes only from the mouths of British gentlemen, as Jamie shrugged out of his dress jacket and, careless as Dominic was meticulous, slung it on the floor. Moving the bear's head out of the way he took Queenie by the shoulders, pulled her down on the bed and then, by the waist, he slid her until she was lying between himself and Dominic.

With Dominic remaining comfortably on his back, hands unmoved from behind his head, a considerable bulge evidencing itself beneath his white trousers, Jamie said, 'The sheila's got no knickers on. Let's take a peep, shall we?'

Once again, Queenie felt material sliding silkily up her legs, the fronts this time, whispering against her stockings. Once again she failed to see it; her eyes were fixed on the underside of the deck of the prow as she relished the sensations coursing through her.

She heard Jamie murmur, 'The sweetest little red-pubed pussy. Will you look at that?'

She was aware of Dominic's grunt, and of the bed creaking as the Englishman moved on to his side, resting on an elbow, watching Jamie slide down her body. The fingers of both of Jamie's hands hooked into the bare flesh of her inside thighs, above the stocking tops. He parted them, and ducked his head down into her bush, wet tongue probing.

With a short, sharp intake of breath, Queenie opened her legs still further, drew up her knees and raised her head to catch only a glimpse of this oh-so-sweet invasion, before Dominic was upon her. Closing in, the Englishman wrapped a hand behind her swept-up hair, pulling her lips on to his while his other hand slipped beneath the low-cut top of her dress and cupped and caressed a breast whose nipple was already hard.

Served thus, Queenie grunted into Dominic's mouth as one of her hands found the top of Jamie's head and the other, pressed into the bed by Dominic's thigh, crept up it to discover the bulge in his trousers and close over it.

Fires began to rage within Queenie as Jamie, thoroughly practised pussy-eater, feasted away between her legs, and Dominic, tongue busy within her mouth, found her zipper, eased it open and dragged her dress down until her breasts were free. He broke the kiss to admire them and then, still supporting Queenie's head, with himself on one elbow, he flattened his hand sideways on a breast and squashed it into the other. He began rolling the breasts into one another and over Queenie's chest as he mumbled, 'Freckled tits. Beautiful, freckled tits. Now, isn't that something!'

As Jamie ate on, Dominic unhanded Queenie, sat up, unzipped himself and got out of his trousers and underpants. Mindful of his clothes, even in his libidinous eagerness, he folded the trousers into their creases and laid them carefully at the very edge of the bed before climbing to his knees to face Queenie, his erection, long and slim like himself, swaying through the open front of the bottom of his shirt. With his endearing, crooked smile, below eyes which fired lust, he muttered with a casual nod at Jamie's head, 'That end seems to be engaged. Do you by any chance . . .?'

Queenie's eyes draped over the cock, and she wetted her lips. 'Come here,' she grated, opening her mouth in welcome. Dominic swung a knee over her breasts, tucked a cushion beneath her head and, with it, pulled her face on to his penis. Rucking up his shirt above his pubic hairs, bunching it in one hand, she slid her lips over his glans and took half the length of his cock into her mouth, flicking her tongue on it, sucking hard, making a slurping sound as he heaved his hips and she lifted his heavy balls in the palm of her hand as if weighing them.

Queenie in paradise! She lets go of the shirt and it tumbles around Dominic's cock. Her hands slide up the backs of his thighs and over the rise of hairless buttocks which they fervently grasp, while her feet, in their Gucci evening shoes still, find their way over Jamie's broad shoulders to meet in the middle of his back, where they cross. Her eyes, drooping, drift back and forth from Dominic's ribald expression to his penis, slipping in and out between her lips, while his hips and her head both rock greedily. Down between her wide-apart, raised thighs, her view of it blocked by Dominic's belly, Jamie brings her close to climax with his busy, busy tongue, a hand beneath him inside his open zipper.

'Time to fuck, my lady,' she hears, muffled, the breath of the words tickling the insides of her thighs. Engrossed in her fellatio, Queenie experiences the slightest pang of regret that Jamie's extended cunnilingus has come to an end. Jamie shuffles on his knees between her legs and shoves his trousers and underpants down his thighs. Still unable to see, Queenie feels, as she sucks on, first one foot, then the other, being lifted and hooked over the Australian's shoulders. Spreading her thighs wide so that his penis is lowered almost to her pussy, he raises her buttocks off the bed with both hands, and like that he impales her as she grunts into her mouthful of cock. It is a lurid scene, only missing mirrors for Queenie to enjoy the full sight as well as the orgiastic sensations of what is being done to her, of what she is doing. Her shoes and stockings are still on as, indeed, is her dress, rucked in a scruffy heap over her belly and spread on either side of her over the bed. One man, a hand behind the cushion which supports her head, the other hand tucking up the front of his shirt, is steadily fucking her face, whilst another, pants and trousers at his knees, kneels just two feet away from him, facing his back, while he fucks her pussy, her legs raised high, feet hooked on his shoulders. Both men are wearing their evening bows; it is the stuff of pure porn, except that it is very real, and Queenie, doubly served, rides a superb sexual high.

The licentious trio continue their activities with no alteration in position, everyone supremely content with their part in the tableau, as all three steadily, inexorably, approach orgasm, and the only thing which does change is the speed of their coupling. Jamie is tilted to one side so that he is able both to partially observe the sucking of his friend and lech at the sight of his own cock plunging in and out of Queenie's coppery pussy. His hands clenched tight beneath the soft flesh of Queenie's buttocks, he raises them higher as a final plunge fully impales her and semen begins to spurt, whilst Queenie clutches Dominic's tight bottom, pulling his cock deep within her mouth as his sperm hits the back of her throat.

With come flooding both her mouth and pussy at the same time, Queenie flies into a mind-shattering orgasm of her own, swallowing sperm as her legs and hips tense into rigidity. Her feet tightly clamp Jamie's head by the ears and, with both cocks spurting their final drops, so intense is her orgasm that she almost faints away.

Dominic keels over, slick, glistening penis sliding from Queenie's lips. He falls across the bearskin, a hand flopping on the bear's head and its adornment of Queenie's knickers, as Jamie sinks back on his haunches, staring with glazed eyes and slack mouth between Queenie's spread, stockinged thighs, where her pussy oozes his juice. Her feet remain on his shoulders, though they no longer hurt his ears, and her eyes are tightly closed. There is a look of wanton, wicked contentment on her face; sperm trickles from one corner of her mouth. As Jamie, with a massive sigh, falls sideways in the opposite direction to Dominic, Queenie's feet go with his shoulders and her tumbling legs twist her on to her side.

The three of them lay where they fell, replete, for long minutes until Jamie said, his words, because of their typical lack of sense of occasion, bringing a crooked smile to Queenie's lips. 'I need a beer. My throat's as dry as a virgin's twat!'

Unhooking Queenie's foot from his neck he swung his legs off the bed. 'Anyone else?'

'Good and cold,' said Dominic, languidly.

'Coming up.'

'Please,' said Queenie, watching him pulling up his pants and trousers, wondering why on earth he didn't simply take them off. But he only buttoned his trouser band together, leaving the belt loose and the zipper undone: the sound of Sonny Rollins floated into the room as he left it to fetch the beers.

'How was it for you, Lady Granville?' asked Dominic with a lazy grin, his fingers absently slipping beneath the crotch of Queenie's knickers on the bear's head. 'Did you make it?'

Queenie, on her back again, leaving her wrecked dress in its lewd pile, muttered, to the ceiling. 'I made it.' She shuddered. 'Oh, I made it all right!'

Jamie reappeared with three cans of San Miguel lager. He closed the door with his foot. 'Girl could catch her death of cold like that?' he observed as he stripped the ring from one and handed it to her.

The tin was icy to the touch. 'No glass?' she asked.

'You want a glass, you know where the bar is.' He tossed a can to Dominic as Queenie shrugged and put hers to her lips.

'The perfect Aussie host, dear Jamie,' Dominic remarked as he opened his beer. 'Manners of the outback!'

Taking a slug of beer, Jamie smacked his lips. Then he said, 'Sorry, Queenie. Nick's right. Do you want a glass?'

'It's all right.' She tilted the beer down her throat, enjoying its refreshing coldness. 'It makes a change when men are rough on me.' She ran an eye over his trousers. 'Going somewhere?'

Picking up the challenge, with a level stare at her crotch, he said, the words managing to thrill her, 'I'm going to have another poke!'

'You'd be better off getting out of your knickers then, not into them, wouldn't you?' she countered.

'This sheila takes the flaming biscuit!' he remarked, to Dominic. 'All right then, I will.'

He undressed completely, leaving his clothes where they fell. Naked, he tilted the beercan, upending it over his mouth until it was empty, while Queenie admired his massive body and formidable set of family jewels. Watching her watching him, he made a show of crushing the can in his big fist, then he went to fetch another. When he came back, Dominic had shifted position. He was sitting up on the bed. Beer-can in one hand, he was toying with Queenie's breast with the other.

'Can't wait to get back at it, mate?' said Jamie.

'Merely doodling, old lad.' Dominic twiddled a nipple. Queenie wriggled. 'That's nice.'

'I'm fascinated with her freckles,' said Dominic.

Jamie chuckled. 'Sure you are.'

Pursing his lips, the Englishman suddenly poured a little lager over one breast. As it trickled down to her belly, Queenie shivered and laughed. 'Ouch! That's freezing!'

Leaning half over her, Dominic, a hand denting the mattress on the other side of her, briefly sucked her wet nipple. Then he licked beer from her upper belly, while Jamie looked on with a lurid grin splitting his face.

'Tastes better like that?' asked the Australian.

'You bet.' Dominic bunched down the dress material and poured a little pool of lager into her navel. He tongued it out as Queenie giggled. She was not yet turned on again but her libido, enjoying this silly game, stirred.

Jamie locked the door, muttering something about the steward. Then he said, 'How come I'm the only one around here bare as a new-born babe? Why don't you strip her, Nick?'

'Good idea,' agreed Queenie. 'This dress is getting ruined.' Sitting up, she bent forward, stretching her arms, the half-empty beer-can in one hand in front of her. 'Why not do as the man suggests?'

Moments later, the dress off and lying in a heap on top of Jamie's jacket, Dominic unclipped a suspender. 'I thought you men preferred a girl with stockings on?' Queenie commented, as he removed a shoe and stripped one silk stocking carefully down her leg.

'Sure, for appetisers,' said Jamie, sitting on the edge of the bed, happily guzzling beer.

'A body like yours has got to be nude sooner or later.' Dominic took his time with the other shoe and stocking, then he sat back and admired her. 'And what a body. My God!'

'Not bad, is it?' said Jamie. 'You should see her and her girlfriend naked together. Now, that's something to write home about!'

'Lucky sod.' He ran his eyes lecherously over Queenie from top to toe. 'He had you both did he?'

'Together, old sport.' Jamie grinned fleetingly. 'Together.'

'And you mean you didn't tell him?' asked Queenie, amazed. 'As I understood it, the first thing a man does after an episode like that is boast to his pals about it.'

'They're usually the liars. Anyhow, what do I need to boast for? I get my oats all the time.'

'And if that's not boasting, I don't know what is,' observed Dominic. He clambered off the bed and unbuttoned his dress shirt. Meticulous as before, he hung it over his jacket. Confronted with the two men without a stitch on, large penises – Dominic's as long as Jamie's but slimmer – flaccid, Queenie dampened her lips, inner excitement quickly building.

Dominic climbed on the bed and squatted cross-legged facing her, frankly probing her body with his eyes, making her keenly aware of her nudity. Her earrings were swaying slowly back and forth with the up-and-down motion of the ship. 'Why don't you let your hair down?' suggested

41

Dominic. 'It's lovely as it is, but I bet you're even more gorgeous with it loose.'

'All right.' Pleased with his words, feeling utterly feminine, Queenie obliged. Her hair cascaded in rolling tresses over her shoulders. She tossed the clips on to her dress. 'Better?'

'Absolutely stunning.' Dominic ran a hand through the shining red locks then let it fall to the swell of her buttocks.

'You're spoiling the chick,' Jamie commented.

'I want to be spoiled.' Queenie looked from one man to the other from under lowered lashes. 'Christ, two of you, that's special!' She had hardly moved from the position she had adopted for Dominic to strip off her dress; she was leaning forward, shoulders hunched slightly, breasts hanging deliciously. Her legs, fractionally apart, were straight in front of her. One hand rested on a knee as the other brought the beer-can to her lips.

Shifting close to her, Dominic slipped one hand around her back and under her arm to a breast while he cupped his other from the side, gentling them both. 'Do you do this sort of thing often?' he asked. 'I mean, making love with two men?'

'Not as often as I'd like.' She smiled to herself as she put the empty can on the bearskin rug, next to the stuffed head. 'It's ... it's really something else, you know? But you'd have to be a girl to understand.'

Dominic jiggled her breasts, lifting first one then the other, fingers and thumbs toying with the hardening nipples. 'Funny thing,' he said. 'I've never, and I mean, but never, met a pretty, upper-class English girl who wasn't horny as hell!'

Jamie snorted. 'Come on sport. Sometimes I swear you British think you invented sex!'

'You mean we didn't?' said Queenie. 'I thought we did!' Her voice had gone husky, the fibres inside her were being stoked by Dominic's playing with her breast. She was yearning for whatever was to be next.

'Well, just so long as you think you did, why don't you go ahead and get this up?' Jamie tossed his empty San

Miguel can to the carpet and got on his knees at her side, thrusting his hips at her face. She stared at his genitals for seconds, lips slightly apart, slid her eyes up his body to his and, staring steamily into them, found his glans with her tongue and drew his warm, soft penis into her mouth.

Jamie grunted appreciation, a hand slipping through her hair to find the back of her neck. 'Christ, I love it when it's soft in there,' he muttered.

'And not when it's hard, old man?' said Dominic mildly as he played on with Queenie's breasts.

'Shut it, Nick, will you?' He pulled Queenie's head tight into his groin. 'Oh, fuck. Jesus, this chick gives head better than a pro!'

Rapidly, Jamie's cock grows to its full proportions between Queenie's sweet lips, as she squeezes his heavy, hairy balls. No longer able to contain all of it in her mouth, she slides her lips back and forth over half of it, trailing saliva over it with her tongue, revelling as always with this giving of head, this ancient art which makes a woman who enjoys it feel sexually in harmony with the man, and performing which turns her on every bit as much as it does him.

'I said I was gonna have another poke. I'm gonna poke you now!' The words, leaden with need, grated through Jamie's teeth as he backed his penis out of Queenie's mouth. 'Excuse me, Nick.' Taking her by the shoulders he heaved her on to her side and laid on the bed facing her, his erection digging into her belly. Lifting her thigh, he draped it over his, slid her up his body a fraction, dragged the other thigh under his and fisted the head of his cock into her wet and waiting pussy.

Dominic, who had keeled over with Queenie, still had hold of her breasts from behind her, and she was aware of his erection rising against a buttock. Jamie's powerful, initial vaginal thrust brought a gasp to her lips.

Jamie fucks Queenie with slow, piston-like strokes, her green-painted nails are raking his broad back, her eyes are closed, her cheek is crushed into his shoulder, while Dominic, crowding into her, pulls her back into his chest with her tits, strains his groin at her buttocks, wriggling it, using her bare bottom to bring himself to full hard-on. The body heat of the two rampant males engulfs her as Jamie's rutting becomes more determined and Dominic plunders her breasts, squeezing roughly but not enough to hurt, his erection flattened upwards between the crack of her buttocks and his belly, jerking it there as if it, too, is inside her. But then he eases her hips away from her, one hand leaves her breast and a saliva-soaked finger finds its way to her bottom hole, working the tip in, wetting it. Queenie is too far gone on this sexual ride to go cold, but she does not want this, and as he whispers raunchily, 'You like a sandwich, Queenie? You want me up your arse?' she moved her mouth away from Jamie's shoulder to mutter, 'No. Please. I don't like it. Please.'

She can feel his disappointment in the way his hand stops moving on her breast and his body goes very still. Seconds later his cockhead slides down her buttocks and she thinks that he is going to bugger her despite her plea. She steels herself, resigned to it, but the glans, pausing only a second at the rear entrance, slips on and down and under until it reaches her pussy, finding room for itself there, cramming under the underside of Jamie's cock.

Jamie's pounding suddenly ceases as his friend's penis slides further up against his own. He protests, a strange, almost fearful note in his voice. 'Hey, what's this, mate? I ain't no fucking queer.'

'Neither am I,' grunts Dominic. He pants his words as he heaves his penis all the way in. 'She wanted to be spoiled. There's no greater way.'

Queenie, beautifully filled, silently agrees, but she fears Jamie is going to pull out of her, that his macho Aussie self is horrifically affronted with the experience of another piece of male equipment sliding tightly against his own. 'Let him, please let him?' she murmurs into his ear. She pokes the tip of her tongue into it, then she tries to further inflame him with dirt-talk. 'It's so fucking marvellous, two big, hot, dirty dicks up my cunt at once. Go on, fuck me, both of you. Do me. Fuck me, you filthy bastards!'

Jamie has been in retreat. His glans, tucked in her threshold hesitates, he heaves his hips once more and both cocks are rammed hard up her, stretching her magnificently, bringing incredible fires to her belly. Despite her encouragement in this act, she has never indulged it before and she sobs into Jamie's shoulder with the sheer, ruttish delight of a pussy sandwich in which, crushed between the strong, sweating men, she is hardly able to move.

They find a rhythm, the penises sliding up and down with regular, pumping movements against each other, balls bumping and colliding as they cross, Jamie's cock rubbing her clitoris, Dominic's exciting her G-spot, this twin fuck-machine thoroughly, utterly, stuffing her, bringing her to unimagined heights – to which the very idea that two cocks are in her cunt at once, two powerful handsome men are screwing her at once adds even more bawdy intoxication.

Queenie's teeth nip into Jamie's shoulder, her nails claw his back, the inside of her foot rides up and down his shin as she is rocked towards climax between two men on a bed in a boat which itself rocks the three of them, timbers creaking, bodies sweaty, the air filled with gasps and groans and grunts, Dominic's groping hands slippery between her tits and Jamie's chest. Jamie's fingers hooked into her buttocks and stretching them wide apart, offering that little hole which she had been so loath to give, Dominic's thighs bouncing up against his friend's hands.

The Rabelaisian beast writhes in a climactic series of jerks, Jamie shouts as his sperm floods and mingles within Queenie with that of Dominic, mixing with her own seeping juices – and both Queenie's teeth and her nails, without her being the slightest aware of it, draw Jamie's blood.

They are still. Unnaturally so except for the heaving of their chests and the pumping of their pulses. The men do not uncouple and Queenie lies squashed between them, vaguely aware of the shrinking of their cocks within her, of their semen oozing out of her and on to the top of a thigh, of their thumping heartbeats, of hers, of the sweat and the earthy smell of them, of the fact that this climax might well have been the greatest orgiastic experience of her life; of the certainty that she will be seeking such a mind-blowing experience again – and again.

Five full minutes pass by, to the sound of their breathing and of the sea breaking gently over the bows of the boat. With a soft grunt, Jamie rolls away on to his back and opens his eyes. He blinks. He becomes aware of a stinging sensation at his shoulder, sees the little curtain of blood. 'Jesus,' he mutters, wetting the ball of his thumb and smearing it over the teeth marks. Then 'Jesus!' again, louder, but he languidly smiles.

Dominic releases Queenie's warm, damp breasts. He pulls his limp, wet length of penis out of her and moves away. 'Shit, do I need another drink,' he says, and gets off the bed.

'Me too, mate,' Jamie agrees.

Queenie sighs, running her hands down the front of her body, where the perspiration is drying. 'I don't know whether to drink it or bath in it!'

They are drained, completely spent, and somehow now there is a great camaraderie in their nakedness, as if what they have just done has brought them further together.

'Was that ever dirty!' comments Jamie, as he strips the ring from his can.

Queenie stares hard at him, sipping her beer, considering. Then she shakes her head. 'No. No, it wasn't,' she says. 'It was wonderful. It was a fantastic, perfectly shared experience.'

'It was?'

'She's right, you know. It was. It was just great, agrees Dominic.

'Yeah. I guess when I think about it, you're both right.' Jamie seems both amazed and puzzled. 'It was okay, wasn't it?' He throws back some beer. 'I never did it before.'

'Neither did I,' says Queenie.

'Nor I,' Dominic confesses.

All three of them laugh aloud, but a little nervously, as if they have just discovered how to split the atom.

# 3

# In and Out of Luk

... I thought my readers might be interested in an extract
from the notes Queenie left me to work from. In the case
of the threesome between Queenie, Coco and Jamie, I had
the Polaroids to guide me – and titillate me madly, I have
to confess! – but as far as that second steaming encounter
was concerned I was obliged to weave my imagination
around Queenie's notes. Of course I had the photos of
Jamie, which helped – and let me tell you he was quite as
big as claimed! It is fortunate for me that Queenie does
not confine her notes to straightforward interviews, most
of which she conducts with a tape-recorder anyway. She
writes sketchy descriptions of scenery, of people and, most
important for me, of sex. The way she writes about sex is
most odd, a sort of personalised shorthand. Well, you will
see ...

... pointed bed, prow of boat, on it bearskin w/head.
Jittery me wants F with both men. J kisses me. Skirt
up, knicks down, D on bed, watching. Knicks over
bearhead, J makes joke. 3 Bs, Mummy B, Daddy B,
Kinky B! D gets my tits out, gropes, J goes down on
me. Wonderful! D offs trousers (v. careful to put in
creases!) I blow D with J eating me, J fs me good,
comes in me, D comes in mouth. Nice! Cold S.
Miguels. J strips naked, D sips beer from my tits &

belly, all get nude. J Fs me again from side w/D behind me, groping. D wants to bugger me, me no like, so stuffs it in pussy with J's dick. Unbelievable sensations! All climax like that – first time for the 3 of us!

... My version is somewhat longer, of course – otherwise we should have a short story instead of a book. Any of you who has read my own adventures in the Frannie series will be aware that this particularly delicious form of sexual sandwich, where two men penetrate the lady's vagina at once, has happened to me personally on more than one occasion. Therefore I consider myself fully qualified to describe the emotions and physical sensations which accompany such a salacious act. (And do I adore it!)

Coco, more or less recovered from her seasickness the following morning, managed breakfast. Then the two of them commenced the task they were aboard for, making themselves known to, and friendly with, the passengers. Queenie interviewed two of them. Coco took some photographs. However, the making of the actual article for *Madame* barely concerns this book. As I mentioned at the outset, the book is about the string of remarkable side events, in particular the sex, which accompanied it.

We catch up with our lovely heroines early in the evening of the second day of the trip ...

'It quite possibly would never have happened had you been there,' Queenie observed, as she pulled a very thin jersey-wool sweater over her head and tucked it into black, satiny slacks.

Coco, dressed for the evening in a beautifully-tailored red Valentino suit, watched Queenie straighten the jersey, the shape of her nipples clearly defined beneath it. 'Lucky old you,' she commented. 'I had much the same experience once in Thailand. Incredible: two Frenchmen. But I've never been close to is since. I think most guys are shy of it.'

'I thought Jamie was going to back off. He froze for a moment when it started. Well, one man's thing in intimate contact with another man's like that. Kind of smacks of homosexuality, and you know what macho-man Jamie's like on that subject.'

'But he didn't back off.'

'No.' Queenie grinned as she fastened a gold belt, made of dozens of gold coins linked together in three rows by chains, around her waist. 'I talked him into staying in me after that moment's hesitation.'

'Dirty talk, I'll bet.'

'Sure. Then he really got at it. Went quite wild, he did.' She pirouetted. 'How do I look?'

'Belt's a bit crooked at the back. C'mere.' As she straightened the chains, Coco said, 'But, surely, it must have had some sexual effect on them? I mean the two cocks tight in you like that, rubbing up and down against each other? I know it did on my Frenchmen, although I think they were a bit on the gay side anyway.'

Queenie frowned and turned to face her. 'I suppose it must, when you come to think of it. They both had massive orgasms, and together.'

'For sure they can't have no female genes in them – isn't it true we all have genes of the opposite sex? And look at us. I wouldn't be without my male genes for the world!'

Smiling, Queenie kissed her lightly on the cheek. She dipped a hand briefly inside her jacket to caress a breast, as she said, 'Too right! But you can bet your life Jamie would never admit to having even a single female gene in his make-up.'

'God, how I'd like to get it on with them like that. Especially since the way you've described Dominic. He sounds terrific.'

'He would. But I doubt if Jamie would do it again.'

'Why do you say that?'

'My guess is that he's going to brood about it a lot, decide there was definitely something bordering on the gay about it, get scared and refuse to get himself in such a situation again.'

Coco laughed. 'Are you a psychologist now?'

'I believe I know my men. Anyway, we'll find out sooner

or later, will we not?' She picked up her handbag. 'Let's go and enjoy a bit of a flutter before dinner.'

The casino was, as ever, busy and animated. Coco took along her camera in case any interesting pictures presented themselves, and it got her into a certain amount of unpleasantness, leading eventually to an extraordinary end to the night. The two of them were having a modest battle with a blackjack dealer – having discovered that here they played the Chinese way: that is, whoever has the highest bet gets to call the cards – when they became aware of growing excitement at the craps table.

As they both lost their bets, a shout went up from the dicing gamblers, sure sign that someone had hit a lucky streak. Leaving Queenie to play both their places, Coco took her Nikon to the table. The big, unsavoury Londoner known as Masters was rolling the dice; there were several piles of high-denomination chips on the 'Win' line in front of him. As is the case with seasoned gamblers, people all around the table were going along with him: a dangerous time for the house. As Coco squeezed herself between them, the man rolled his fourth 'natural' winner, an eleven, doubling almost everyone's money.

Coco studied the man's pudgy white face. His flat grey eyes registered little emotion as, leaving his entire bet to ride, he tossed the dice down the table and they produced yet another eleven. A cheer went up around him, but he raised only the suggestion of a smile, which melted as soon as it appeared. Leaving half the bet to ride, he rolled again. This time they showed four and five. He would need to roll another nine to win, and should he roll a seven on the way he would lose.

Focusing her lens on him and the people on either side of him, she waited for him to roll and for the dice to come to a stop, determined to capture the emotions on those faces when they did. She fired the shot, with flash, the instant the croupier called. 'Seven, a loser.' The faces, except for that of the Englishman, fell. He glared angrily down the table at her. 'Heh, you . . .' he snapped, his voice harsh and rough, 'what's the bleedin' idea?'

'I'm sorry,' Coco responded, alarmed. 'It was just a photo.'

'Just a bloody photo, is it?' He pushed his way from the table and stalked around it to her side. 'You wrecked my luck with your fuckin' camera,' he fumed.

She blinked at the violence of his language. 'But I didn't take the picture until the dice had stopped rolling. In any case,' she objected, 'what if I had? It's nutty to suggest that a camera can affect dice.'

He seemed to relax fractionally. It was as if his flat little grey eyes had noticed her sexiness for the first time. 'Gamblers are superstitious – you should know that.'

'I'm sorry you lost,' said Coco.

'I 'ad a fair run,' he said grudgingly. His next words were addressed to her breasts which, encased in a lacy white blouse, jutted fetchingly through the open front of her red jacket. 'You 'n' your girlfriend, what's it you're up to then? I've seen you takin' pictures, 'er askin' questions.'

'We're putting together an article for a magazine. About the sort of people who take a trip like this – what motivates them, the places the boat visits, that sort of thing.'

His eyes narrowed. 'Magazine? What magazine?'

'*Madame.*'

'Yankee glossy, no? Big?'

'Yes.'

He seemed to be about to flare up again. There was an edge of menace to his words, a glare in his eye. 'I don' want my face in no fuckin' magazine, got it?'

'Asking nicely helps.'

'Yeah, well . . .' His eyes pigged on her breasts again. There was something especially nasty about the man, she decided. 'Maybe I'll ask nicely la'er. Why don' you 'n' your friend 'ave a drink with me after dinner? Right now I've go' a stack of chips to look after.'

Not finding the prospect of this exactly wonderful, Coco nevertheless decided on discretion. 'If you like. We're planning to eat about nine.'

'Fine. See you la'er.'

Back at the blackjack table, Coco was pleased to find that

51

Queenie had been winning on both places. She told her about the Englishman. 'Weird,' she said. 'First he rants about me spoiling his luck, then he gets belligerent about his photo, after which he invites us for a drink.'

Queenie glanced across the casino towards the craps table where Masters, no longer the dice shooter, was laying bets with his typical lack of emotion. She wrinkled her nose in distaste. 'I think you can make my excuses. Tell him it was hate at first sight.'

'Whatever happened to your nose for a story? If ever there was one, it's hiding behind him.'

'Sure. And he's going to spill it to me, isn't he? Remember Jamie's words about him? Taciturn bastard – isn't that what he said? Forget it. Anyway, I'm not looking for a scoop, I'm trying to put together an intelligent story.' The dealer hit her fourteen with a seven. 'Look at that. Every one a winner.' But then the girl flipped her down card to reveal an ace and blackjack. 'Shit!'

'So, you're planning to leave me alone with that slob?'

'Not if you're afraid of him.'

Coco laughed. 'You should know me better.'

But she was not alone with the man. The Chinese hooker – if, indeed, hooker was what she was – was with him, and the girl was stunning. She was Coco's size, with hair just as black and shiny and straight, but very much shorter, and she wore a silk emerald-green cheongsam slit high up a bare, shapely, suntanned leg. Her name was Luk, which could hardly have suited the companion of a gambler better. After less than five minutes in her company Coco had assessed her as highly intelligent. Curiously, her English was not the usual sing-song variety spoken by the Chinese of Hong Kong, but something that seemed to be a cocktail of Australian and American, pleasant to listen to, highly unusual.

The two young women got on famously with one another, whilst Masters – taciturn indeed – contributed very little to the conversation. At least he wasn't being unpleasant.

As she sipped a powerful brew which bore the same name as Luk's dress, a 'cheongsam', its alcoholic base gin and white crème de menthe, Coco ventured a leading question. 'Are you a professional gambler, Max?' she asked. 'I mean, is that what you do for a living?'

'Life's a gamble,' was his unhelpfully grunted reply.

'Sure. But do you do anything else?' she insisted.

'I mind my own business, don' I? And I ask photographer birds, in the nicest possible way, if they'd let me 'ave the negatives of any shots they've taken of me.' He was not looking at her as he said this; his eyes were darting all around the softly-lit Thirties-style bar.

'Well, yes, you can have the negative of course.' Incautiously she added, 'But why would you want it?'

A shade of annoyance crossed his eyes as they swivelled to hers. 'Don't needle me, eh, love? There's a good girl. So maybe I'm a Moslem and I believe you've stolen my soul in the camera.'

Coco took a deep breath. She was getting rattled herself, but, remembering Jamie's advice, she didn't let it show. 'All right. Like I said, you can have the neg just as soon as I've developed it.'

'So you do your own stuff?'

'Usually.'

'When do you deliver?'

'It'll be in today's batch. Tomorrow, some time.'

'Don't le' me down, eh?'

'Curious, that Moslem and his soul stuff, no?' said Luk. 'Ain't that more or less what you try to do with a picture? Capture the soul?'

'In a way, I suppose it is, yes.' Coco shot her an appreciative look, which lingered. Suddenly she found herself fancying this girl, who could not have been more than twenty. 'You enjoy photography?'

'Yeah. Ain't no flaming good, though.'

'Don' forge' your promise,' Masters interrupted, still on about the photograph. 'I ge' the negative tomorrow, and no 'ard feelings?'

'No hard feelings, no.'

'Good.' His eyes took their time wandering over first Luk's curves, then Coco's. 'Coupla peaches, you two together.' He nodded at the half-full glasses. 'Let's put these away and 'ave some more. Ge' a bi' merry.'

Just how it was that she found herself, some while later, in their cabin with Masters and Luk, Coco was not terribly sure. She knew only that three – or was is four? – cheongsams had gone to her head, that the furthest thing in her mind was the prospect of any sort of dalliance with the Englishman; the idea was repulsive. But she remembered making a somewhat tipsy verbal advance to Luk, which had been very much reciprocated.

It was a largish cabin with a double bed, nowhere near as grand as Coco's suite, but very comfortable. Several Van Gogh prints added nice splashes of colour. 'Warm in here,' Coco said, as she watched Masters opening a bottle of Krug, which she felt sure was going to put an end to any effort of sobriety on her part.

Luk took the cue – and the opportunity. 'Give me your jacket.' She moved behind Coco as she shrugged out of the padded shoulders. Taking one of the shoulders in her hand, she swept the back of Coco's hair to one side and surprised her by planting a kiss on the nape of her neck. Coco shuddered at the sensuous warmth of it. Luk removed her lips and whispered in her ear, 'That's what you came here for, ain't it?'

'Maybe.' The word caught in Coco's throat.

Taking the jacket off, Luk draped it over one arm. Her hand stole around Coco's body to close in on a breast, over her white lace blouse. 'You're a right darling, you know that?' she murmured, as she gentled the breast. Nosing away Coco's long hair, she kissed her neck again, sending little pleasure thrills up and down her spine. This young Chinese girl clearly knew all about making love to her own sex.

Filling champagne glasses as he watched the two of them with half an eye, Masters remarked. 'That's wha' I like to see. Wastin' no time gettin' acquainted, are we?'

'She's a real honey, Max,' said Luk as she pressed her crotch into Coco's behind, her hand straying from one breast to the other.

'Sure. Bu' right now it's bubbly time. Break it up, kids – we've got all nigh'.' He held two glasses towards them. Luk treated Coco's bra-less breasts to a final affectionate squeeze before letting it go. She went to a wardrobe to hang the jacket.

Quite certain of the raunchiness of her feelings for Luk, but harbouring severe doubts about the presence of Masters, just about the crudest example of masculinity she had ever been in the company of, Coco accepted from him a glass which brimmed champagne, whilst wondering fleetingly just what the hell she was doing there.

Clinking his glass against hers, Masters leered at her before gulping down the Krug as if it were beer. 'My Luk, she likes a pretty chick,' he said as his girlfriend, whore, whatever her station in life was, picked up her glass from the bar. 'Don't you, love?'

'I – I'm not really sure if I should be here,' muttered Coco.

Masters chuckled. 'You weren't exactly fightin' 'er off you.'

'No.' Nervously, her hand faintly trembling, Coco tipped champagne down her throat. She studied Masters flatly, trying to keep distaste from her expression. Overweight. Unappetising. Gross, even. 'It's just that . . .'

'In the way, am I? Well, I ain't leavin'!'

With a grin, Luk linked her arm in his. 'Don't bother your pretty head about him. He's kind of a sweety once you get to know him. My koala bear.'

'She don' fancy me, that's obvious.' He unhooked his arm from Luk's and let himself down into a chair with a grunt. 'That's all righ', darlin' – I won' lay a pinkie on you, if you don' wan' – that's a promise.' He leered. I'll jus' watch, won' I?'

Luk took hold of Coco's free hand. 'He's okay, I promise.'

Emptying her glass, glad to be light-headed, needing to be, Coco said, 'Can I have another?'

'Sure thing.'

Watching her pouring the champagne, Coco felt once again how the brush of her lips and the touch of her hand on her breasts had been. The girl's dress was slit almost to her knickers, the smooth brown flesh of her thigh temptingly exposed. Realising suddenly that not even the presence of Masters was going to keep her away from Luk, Coco took the filled glass, and smiled. For a second, as Luk smiled gently back, Coco saw two of her, one image sliding slightly over the over. She blinked the girl back into focus, then was careful to take only a small sip from her glass.

Two smouldering sets of oriental eyes, Luk's more slanted than Coco's, met and locked, the excitement of anticipated sex lurking there.

'Gonna ge' on with the show, then?' Masters' clumsily mouthed words went some way towards breaking the spell, but not all of it.

'Shut your fucking trap, Max, no?' said Luk, sounding all Australian. Taking Coco's glass from her hand she set it on the table and raised her own glass to Coco's lips, tilting slightly. 'Here's to us,' she murmured, eyes burning into the black depths of Coco's.

The bubbly sparkled down a throat gone suddenly dry. 'To us,' repeated Coco, then her glass joined the other on the table and the two girls fell into each other's arms, hips grinding, breasts squashed against breasts, lips and tongues mingling – while, in his chair, Masters ogled.

Luk felt, smelt, and tasted divine. Coco found herself caught up in such a rising tide of passion that the presence of Masters became only the most minor of irritants. Fingers squeezed bottoms as tongues played with tongues. Breaking the kiss, Coco slid slowly down Luk's body, lips whispering over the green silk cheongsam, pausing to kiss her breasts through it, hands remaining where the kisses had been as she sank to her knees and buried her face between Luk's legs, breathing hot air through the silk as Luk heaved her hips and parted her thighs with a tiny sigh.

Her hands leaving the girl's breasts with a parting

squeeze, Coco slithered them over her buttocks, and on down the back of her legs, until they reached the hem of her dress. She started to pull it up over her knees, but Luk stopped her.

'I'll take it off,' she said.

Coco's hands stole up the backs of warm, firm thighs while Luk took hold of the zipper which ran from neck to hem of the dress and opened it all the way up, bending at the knees to reach the last bit, then straightening and shrugging her shoulders forward so that the silk fell away from them. Pulling her arms out of the cheongsam she dropped it on the carpet behind Coco. Confronted with the spellbinding sight of a minuscule pair of fine lace knickers, tiny flowers woven into the crotch, black pubic hairs curling from under them on to the inside tops of fleshy thighs and a good inch of thick bush above the waistband, Coco dived her head in amongst the flowers as her hands slipped up under the backs of the knickers over warm, taut buttocks.

Luk's knees sagged and parted, her fingers clawing into Coco's hair as she peered down through swaying, naked breasts and a row of shiny beads. She could only see Coco's face as far as the tip of her nose; her mouth, buried between Luk's legs, was again breathing hot air into her crotch, but this time the only barrier to her lips was almost non-existent, and the sensation for Luk was exquisite.

The final barrier was whisked away as Coco rolled the knickers down Luk's thighs, all the way down her legs, and off one foot, leaving them dangling around the other ankle as she wetly traced the tip of her tongue from Luk's knee, slowly up the inside of her thigh, until it reached her pussy where it plunged to Luk's accompanying squeal of delight.

'Jesus fuckin' Christ!' muttered Masters from his chair, eyes pigging, hand clutching at the bulge in his trousers. But, if they heard, neither girl took the slightest notice: Coco engrossed in eating this so-sweet pussy, Luk with her eyes closed grinding away with her hips, almost as if she were riding a penis.

To Coco's surprise and infinite pleasure, Luk quickly reached orgasm. Her hips gave a jerk even more powerful, she produced another of her squeals, then the hips stilled as her thighs, muscles taut, gripped Coco's cheeks and her hands, at the back of Coco's head, held her face for long seconds, jammed tight into her crotch.

As Luk relaxed, muscles slackening, Coco unmouthed her, looking up at her face through her breasts with smouldering eyes, mouth glistening, lipstick smeared.

'Good?' she asked.

Luk's eyes, heavy with contentment, lazily opened. 'Uh huh,' she said. 'Now you.'

She helped Coco to her feet and led her to the bed, where she laid her down. Taking a great deal of time about it, kissing every inch of flesh as it was revealed, she stripped Coco of her clothes until she was naked. Then, kneeling between Coco's spread legs, her buttocks on her heels, she pushed Coco's thighs high and wide, cupped her bottom in both hands, and went down on her.

Coco became vaguely, uncomfortably aware that Masters had left his chair and was now standing over them by the side of the bed. Luk's flickering tongue was doing delightful things to her, but the man's closeness intruded momentarily, very slightly dulling the pleasure. Her eyes slid from the shiny, ebony top to Luk's head to the bulk of Masters – taking in the fact that his unlovely face was bloated with lust, but at least his trousers were still closed – before she screwed them tightly shut and blanked the man out of her mind, as she lost herself in Luk's cunnilingual attentions.

And, God, how this young girl was skilled in the art! While her tongue poked and probed, going deep inside her, stabbing in and out, pausing for her to take Coco's little clitoris between her lips, to nibble it, to suck it, her fingers roved, stroking and pinching the insides of her thighs, slipping inside Coco's pussy beside her tongue, parting her buttocks to titillate her bottom hole.

A few minutes more of such delicious spoiling was too much for Coco. Rolling her head from side to side, she grunted and moaned her orgasm, and went still. Luk, engrossed in what she was doing, bringing herself towards another carnal high by it, kept up her tongue and finger work until Coco, beginning to switch on all over again, opened her eyes and then her arms, and breathed. 'Come up here and kiss me.'

Luk's face slides up over Coco's tight little belly past the diamond mole, tongue trailing saliva, to her jutting breasts, where it pauses and she sucks on each nipple, drawing them into her mouth like a baby. She goes higher, and soft mouths engage as pelvises join. Coco wraps her legs around the back of Luk's thighs. Luk's bottom begins to rock. The two heavy black bushes intermingle as the pubises grind against one another – Luk, moving as if she were a man impaling Coco, bringing pleasure to them both.

But now there is movement by the side of the bed. Coco, riding another sexual high, watches – she cannot help it – with awful fascination as Masters takes off his shoes, clambers out of his trousers, then pulls down and off a big pair of red Y-fronts. He undoes the front of his shirt; from within a mat of hairs at his belly protrudes a fat, stubby erection. He is so like a gorilla that his balls are half buried in a bed of hairs between his thighs. Utterly disagreeable as this man is, it is an erect cock which Coco's eyes have settled on, and it does nothing to detract from the shivers of libidinous excitement which Luk's rocking pelvis and their mingling tongues are bringing her. Taking himself in hand, Masters starts to slowly masturbate. Coco is unable to drag her gaze away, as Luk's love-making brings her closer and closer towards orgasm.

Suddenly Masters leans forward, picks up Coco's hand from where it lies flattened on Luk's buttock and before Coco realises what is happening, he has replaced his own fingers on his penis with hers.

Coco, by now too high on her sexual cloud to be brought down, forces herself to forget who this man is; it is a warm, disembodied erection she had hold of. Her fist begins to jerk on it in time to Luk's bouncing hips. Up to now she has been relishing pure, undefiled pleasure, but for the first time this evening she starts to feel dirty, for the first time what she is doing is dirty, and, belly seething, she acts accordingly. She does a thing which, a very short time ago, she would never have envisaged herself doing, ever. She breaks the kiss and pulls Masters towards her by his hard-on. Grasping her intentions, the man spreads his weight on his beefy hands above the girls' heads, props a knee on the bed, one foot remaining on the carpet and allows his stubby penis to be drawn into Coco's mouth. Luk, her cheek pressed into Coco's, Masters' cock inches away, watches lustfully, her hips grinding faster.

In her not inconsiderable imagination, this cock now has a young and handsome man attached to it. As Coco sucks it, she pulls her legs high up Luk's back, raising her bottom as much as she can, so that Luk's clitoris just succeeds in making contact with her own with each rock of her hips. Luk's mouth opens, she wets her lips, staring longingly at Coco's fellatio. She takes hold of the cock and frees it from Coco's mouth. Masters shifts his hips slightly, and now he is inside Luk's mouth, slowly fucking it as his balls jiggle and roll on Coco's chin and lips, while she runs her tongue over them. From mouth to mouth goes Masters' cock as the girls, climbing the dizzy heights of orgasm, further inflamed by the sucking, the watching, ride their way to mutual, frenzied, climax.

'So wha' abou' me?' complains Masters as the fellatio abruptly ceases and he is left half-kneeling on the bed. The girls, locked in one another's arms, eyes closed, are still.

Luk's eyes stay shut but she mutters lazily, 'Okay. Do it the way you like best, baby.'

Coco feels the bed denting, she hears it creak. Luk's knees, between her own, part her legs more. Except for the gentle, sideways roll of the cabin, there is a moment's stillness. Then Masters grunts, an animal sound produced deep within his throat, three times. Luk whimpers, she makes a noise as if in pain – 'Ow. Owwww!' – and Coco, feeling hot, vaguely unpleasant, breath on her face, opens her eyes on Masters' flabby, white, lust-wrecked face which hovers inches from her own. The head dips, it appears he is about to kiss her; this, in no way can she stomach. Blowing an impersonal cock whilst pretending it belongs to a handsome man is one thing; kissing its ugly owner, and after such a wonderful orgasm, is quite another, unthinkable. She turns her head down as far as she can, burying her lips in her shoulder.

Masters ducks his face into where the ends of Luk's short hairstyle meet her neck. Coco feels his weight, through Luk, as Luk's breasts squash hard into hers and roll them up and down with Masters' rocking motion. Coco, relieved that she has avoided the kiss, raises her head and one shoulder to peer down their three bodies. Masters is jerking his behind, most of his weight on his hands, the slapping of his hips against Luk's rear end releasing some of his heaviness through Luk and into Coco, but not enough to more than slightly crush her. In fact it is curiously pleasant because, whilst Coco lies quite unmoving, Luk heaves on her in this heavy embrace and their crotches are once more slipping and sliding and bumping one another.

As Masters' thighs pull away from the back of Luk's in preparation for another thrust, Coco digs a hand down between her and Luk's bellies, two fingertips reaching for the girl's pussy, eager for a grope of the action. She encounters Masters' cock and prurient thrills course through Coco as her hand reaches further until the tips of the index and second fingers open in a V around it, to become an extension to Luk's pussy.

The Chinese girl raises her head, her mouth seeks out Coco's. As they kiss, Luk forces her hand down between them. She finds Coco's wet pussy and gets a finger inside it, while Coco's free hand strays to her buttock, grasping it close to her fingers and the plunging cock, as aware through her hands of what is happening there as if she were looking directly at it.

With a final heave, almost soundlessly Masters climaxes and immediately rolls away and on to his back. But Coco and Luk are not there yet. With no words, but with what seems to be a telepathic understanding, Luk spins through

61

a hundred and eighty degrees on Coco's body, tongues simultaneously and most voraciously invade pussies, hungrier than they have been yet, during this lustful bawdy evening, and the female lovers sixty-nine themselves to a moaning, squealing, mutual orgasm.

Recovery brings a certain amount of self-doubt to the normally conscience-free Coco as she looks with distaste upon Masters who – flat on his back, hairy belly wobbling, penis shrunk into his pubic forest so that only its circumcised head peeps out – loudly snores.

Luk, catching her expression, following it, wrinkles her pert little nose. 'Horrible, ain't he?' she quietly proclaims. 'But he's just loaded with bread. So is his Chinese mate.'

Ah, then the girl was a whore. Coco wondered how she could have thought otherwise. Climbing off the bed, realising that she was fairly sober once more as she swayed comfortably with the boat, she found her knickers and stepped into them. Luk watched her closely, dark sloping eyes running over her body, ogling her. A whore she might be, but enthusiastically sexy she was as well – at least with women. She may or may not have enjoyed her doggy-fucking; it was possibly only the fact that Coco was under her while it was occurring which had quite so turned her on.

Neither of them spoke until Coco was ready to leave. Then Coco said, her hand on the cabin doorhandle. 'Do it again some time?' She nodded towards the snoring Englishman. 'Without him?'

'Sure, doll,' Luk responded in that funny accent of hers. 'For you, honey, it'll be for free!'

# 4

# Bunking Up

As it slid out of the East China Sea into the huge harbour of Keelung, on the north side of Taiwan, the *Star of Kowloon* hooted noisily. Three short, mournful, double blasts reverberated across the busy waters and around the massive statue of Kuan-Yin, the Goddess of Mercy, which dominated a hill overlooking the harbour.

'What d'you know – we're in China,' said Coco. She was kneeling on a bench seat in their suite, designer jeans stretched tightly over her behind, nose pressed to a rain-streaked porthole.

Queenie grimaced. 'Stinking weather.'

'Keelung means Raindragon. This is Raindragon city where it hardly ever stops. One of the world's wettest places.'

'So what do we do here?'

Coco turned around and propped her back on the porthole, opening the ship's schedule. 'We're here for twenty-four hours. We can take a bus tour down the coast to a place called Hualien, ditto up into the mountains, or we can go into the capital, Taipei.'

Queenie groaned. 'Jesus, buses in this weather? So how far is Taipei?'

'Not far. About thirty kilometres.'

'Let's do that. But forget the bus. We'll hire a car and driver. That way we're free to go where we like – and we're not obliged to get out.'

'We're supposed to be doing an article about these gamblers, remember? That means sticking around with them.'

'I'd prefer to take a break. Anyway, they won't be gambling today; they'll be doing the tourist bit.'

'Whatever you like. Tell you what, let's try and get Jamie to come along. He'll know where to go.'

Queenie smiled. 'That ought to be fun!'

For a while the rain continued to cascade down. With the windows of the hired Mercedes misting up, they might have been almost anywhere, but then, as they wound their way slowly through mountains, heading south-west, a small patch of blue heralded imminent change, and quite suddenly the clouds rolled away. Bright sunshine fell on an ornate, seven-tiered pagoda nestling in a lush and verdant hill, and they could have only been in China.

Taipei, principal city of the Republic of China, presented itself as an instant cultural shock when they were driven along the first of its main thoroughfares. Very straight, it was an incredible jumble of red, green, yellow and blue signs running from top to bottom of the smallish apartment blocks, every one of them, with the exception of the occasional Seiko or other international brand name, in Chinese characters, cloaking the area in mystery.

'Same people,' commented Jamie, between the two girls, his hands cosily resting on one knee of each. 'Not far away, either, but we could be in an entirely different world from Hong Kong.'

'Where are you planning to take us?' asked Coco.

'For lunch in a rather fine restaurant I know. But first, we'll take a stroll around. I thought you'd find it amusing to visit a shê shop – something for you to stick in your article, perhaps.'

' "Shê shop?" What's that – a brothel?' asked Queenie hopefully as she covered the hand on her knee with her own.

He laughed. 'No such flaming luck. Snakes.'

'Snakes? God!'

\* \* \*

'Welcome to Snake Alley,' Jamie announced, ten minutes later. The street was narrow, teeming with people and with not a European face in sight. It had a distinct, pungent smell to it, rather like an Arabian market but less herby. 'Here's where you'll find a bunch of the best-fed mongooses in the world.'

'Shouldn't that be mongeese?' asked Queenie.

'No, Miss Journalist, it's not. Mongooses. Cute little critters.'

They threaded their way along Snake Alley in file, passing many shops which had big iron cages outside, snakes squirming within them. Beside most of these cages was a chained mongoose, lying down, plump, oblivious to the bustle of the passers-by. Jamie stopped where a small crowd was gathering. 'Here,' he said. 'A killing about to happen.'

'I'm not too sure I'm that enthusiastic about it,' said Queenie with a shudder.

'Ain't nothing. Happens the same in the wild.'

Coco clutched her friend's arm. 'He's right. I've seen it before. It's quite quick.' She unclipped her camera case. 'I'll get a few pictures.'

A stir ran through the crowd as a wizened, yellow little man who might have been a hundred years old stooped to open a sliding door in a cage, just a couple of centimetres. A snake slithered free, the door was dropped, and the change in the attitude of the mongoose was immediate and impressive. Its hackles rose, and it displayed its sharp little teeth, before pouncing on the snake, grabbing it behind the head and shaking it like a dog worrying a toy. The fight was short-lived and one-sided; the mongoose had sunk its teeth into the exact spot for a kill first time; the snake was soon dead.

The mongoose, then offered an alternative morsel of food, gave up its prey without protest, and the old man neatly skinned the snake and dropped its body into a boiling pot. He stirred this for five minutes, his rheumy, jaundiced-looking eyes never leaving the liquid, then he set aside his stick and began dipping cups into the brew which he offered to the men in the crowd. Several of them paid him some money for a drink.

'What's the idea of that?' asked Queenie.

'You've heard of Spanish fly?' said Jamie. 'This is a ...'

He was interrupted by the old man offering him a cup of the snake brew, with the extraordinary words, 'Vely nice aphlodisiac. Give you mighty fine election, mistahh!' as he folded a forearm into the upper arm with a suggestive jerk, fist clenched.

Coco giggled. 'Go for it, Jamie!' she exclaimed.

Jamie spoke some words in Chinese, and the old man looked with what might have been the faintest hint of interest from Queenie to Coco, shrugged, then turned away to offer the cup to someone else.

'What did you tell him?' asked Queenie.

With a broad grin, Jamie said, 'I told him no way did I need an aphrodisiac with you two in tow.'

Coco hooked her arm through his. 'Showing off again, big boy!'

'Not half.'

'Where to now?'

'Lunch. Unless you fancy sticking your head inside the shop?'

'What's in there?'

'Someone'll be preparing snake medicine. What you saw was just a show to pull the crowd. The biggest business, apart from food, is medicine. He'll be cutting the creatures up, taking out the gall bladder and liver ... that sort of thing.'

'Trying to put us off our lunch?' Queenie protested. 'Let's go, no?'

The restaurant was in a dusty, colourful alley, narrower even than Snake Alley, and on the first floor, reached by a worn and creaking wooden staircase. They found a table overlooking the street. There was no concession here to Western eating habits, and Jamie and Coco were obliged to give Queenie rudimentary lessons in the use of chopsticks.

During the meal – as Queenie was cursing a crisp shrimp ball which evaded her chopsticks – Jamie exclaimed peering down into the street, 'Well, what do you know? Look who we have here.'

Masters, the big Englishman, leading his equally bulky Chinese friend, Li, was shoving his way through the crowds. They were head and shoulders taller than most other people. Pausing at a doorway nearly opposite the restaurant, they darted furtive glances around before slipping through it.

'What is that place?' asked Queenie. Above the door-frame was one small, faded Chinese character.

'Hell ...' Jamie blinked down at the street. 'That beats all. I reckon, and I think I'm right, that's an opium den.'

'I'll second that,' said Coco, as memories of last night's debauch crowded her mind.

'I'd never have taken Masters for a dope-head,' said Jamie.

'Hang on. Now what on earth is *she* doing?' Coco stretched her neck to get a better view. The startling, black-leather lady of the craps table, dressed now in a fine red leather miniskirt, spiky high heels to match, and a white turtle-necked blouse, had appeared a short way down the street. She was buying a hot biscuit from a stall, but her attention was on the same doorway through which Masters and Li had disappeared. Nibbling the biscuit, she leant back against a shop window, watching the door.

'That is weird,' commented Coco. 'She seems to be following them. Now why would she do that?' Taking her camera from its bag she focused on the woman and took two shots.

'What did you do that for?' asked Jamie.

'Something odd's going on. They may come in useful.'

'Yeah. But it's none of your business, baby.'

'Maybe not. But you never know.' Coco took a third picture and laid the camera down on the table next to her plate, leaving the lens uncapped.

'I warned you on day one, kid.' Jamie covered her hand with his. 'I get some very dodgy characters on my boat. Keep your nose clean.'

Coco shrugged. 'They're only photographs. I mean, nobody knows I've taken them, do they?'

'I do.'

Queenie changed the subject. If Coco was going to take photos, then Coco was going to take photos. Nothing short of strong-arm treatment would stop her, and even then her skills in the martial art of aikido weren't to be ignored. 'Did you give Masters the negative you promised?' she asked.

'Just before we docked.' She smiled. 'I took a second print from it, though.'

'Hell, you're just looking for bother, Coco,' said Jamie. 'Well, I'm done warning you, you nut.' He paused. 'By the way, where are my promised pictures?'

'Done. You can collect them in our cabin any time, porn star!'

As they were finishing up their meal, Masters and Li emerged from the opium den. Coco took more pictures. When they were out of sight, the watching woman slipped through the door. Coco shot yet another picture.

Jamie sighed at her, but did not admonish further. 'What in God's name are they up to?' he said. 'They didn't go in for a smoke; they'd have taken much longer. In any case, no way did they look stoned.'

'And now she's in there,' Queenie added – at the same moment as the woman came out again.

'That was sure some flying visit,' said Jamie.

'How can we be certain it's a dope den?' asked Queenie.

'Why would you want to be certain?'

Queenie tapped her nose.

'Christ, you're as bad as her!' He stared at her. 'If you must, there's only one way to find out.'

'Not me, baby,' said Coco. 'I'm not going in there. Those joints give me the creeps.' She took a sip of her coffee. 'But you two go right ahead. Feel free.'

'Okay, let's do it, Jamie,' said Queenie, rising. 'You don't mind waiting here, Coco?'

'I've got a magazine. But try not to be all afternoon.'

Dope den, indeed, it was. It was like going into a

particularly cheap and dingy hostel, except that the sweet, slightly sticky smell of opium hit them as soon as they were across the threshold. Jamie exchanged words in Chinese with an expressionless man who was sitting behind a brown-painted wooden desk, then he somewhat shocked Queenie by giving the man some money in exchange for two long curved pipes filled with what she presumed was opium. She felt particularly out of her depth, a little scared, and even somewhat wicked as they were shown along a dark, creepy passage and into a narrow room where the stench of opium was at its most powerful. Two facing walls of this room were lined with cubicles, each one fitted out with a mattress, a pillow and a grubby set of curtains. One or two of the curtains were pulled shut; in a few open cubicles men lay back, puffing on pipes, their eyes vacant or closed.

'Welcome to dreamland,' said Jamie, as the doorman disappeared. Nobody seemed to be taking the slightest notice of them.

Suppressing a shudder, Queenie nodded at the two pipes which Jamie held in one hand, by their bowls. 'But you actually bought some of the wretched stuff?'

'Wouldn't have got past the door if I hadn't.'

She looked around. 'Grim, to say the least. I can't really see what we're going to learn here – except that it is what you said.'

'You never know.'

'Am I going to suffer from the effects of passive smok-ing?'

'You might get a bit light-headed if we stick around.'

'But let's stay – just for a little while.'

'So pick a bunk.'

'What?'

'A bunk. It is the custom.'

'I suppose it is, yes.' She glanced at the choices, suddenly realising the implications, with slightly quickening pulse. Lying down on a bed with Jamie. 'Together?'

'How about that?' His eyes ran quickly up and down her form. 'It's going to be a bit of a tight squeeze.'

'It will, won't it? That's nice.' Her gaze fell on a cubicle at waist height with no one below it and a closed curtain above. 'Let's get in there, then.' The cloying, pungent air notwithstanding, this was beginning to be fun. 'You first.'

Jamie needed to bend his knees to cram in the length of his large frame. Once in, his back to the wall, he helped Queenie up. She was wearing a tight, calf-length pencil skirt which made the operation a little tricky – and greatly revealing to anyone who cared to look as she hiked it up. Finally, laughing quietly, she was on her back next to him, staring at untreated planks of pine over their heads. 'Now what?' she whispered. 'We're clearly not going to learn anything about Masters and Li.'

'Now I'm going to have me a couple of puffs.'

'Are you serious?'

'Why not? I've paid for it, haven't I? It won't do any harm. I've had it before.' He stuck a pipe in his mouth, then took it out again. 'Shit. I don't have anything to light it with. Do you?'

'I don't smoke. You know that.'

'You could get me a light.'

'Me? Not me.' She paused. 'And you can't get out now.'

'Forget it. It's not that great an idea. I'll take a few really deep sniffs at the air instead.'

She giggled. 'You know, I do believe I'm feeling a bit heady.'

'Not surprising, is it?' He stared at her. His knee was lying sideways over hers, her skirt above them. 'So, now what?'

She stared levelly back, knowing full well what was crossing his mind, since the notion was very firmly in her own. She took the two pipes from his hand and tucked them under the pillow at the head of the bunk, then she dropped a hand lightly on his upper arm. 'I haven't a clue, have you?'

He pressed closer to her, his hand sliding between two buttons of her blouse and on to the flat of her belly. 'No. But we could, you know, cuddle up a bit.'

'In here? Really, Mister Bond, what do you take me for?'

'How about randy bitch?'

'Now you're talking!' His hand suddenly felt as if it were burning into the flesh of her belly. She reached behind her head. 'I'll close the curtains. Wouldn't want to shock the neighbours.'

Then she rolled into his arms, her lips hungrily finding his, a sudden fury of desire unleashed within her by his closeness in this eerie, degenerate place. He broke his mouth from hers as his fingers fumbled with the zip at the back of her skirt. 'Here's something to put in your *Madame* article,' he muttered. 'You can call it, "How I was fucked by an Aussie gambling-boat owner in a Chinese opium den". That'll sure sell magazines.'

'Don't use that dirty word,' she said, as she twisted her hip from the mattress so that he could pull her skirt down more easily.

'What dirty word?' He dragged the skirt over her knees, as she kicked off her shoes.

'Aussie.'

'Aussie? That's a dirty word?'

'I hope so.' She began to unbutton his Levis as her skirt came off, and the balls of two of his fingers pressed into the flimsy knickers at her crotch. She shivered. 'I fucking hope so!'

That huge penis of his was already rock hard. As she opened his jeans wide to get it out, she briefly wondered if it hurt to have it confined by the tight, heavy denim. Then it was free, warm and welcome in her palm, throbbing and eager for action. 'Hello, Arnold!' she muttered happily.

He started to laugh, but it was choked off by a sigh as she slid her head down his shirt, flicked her tongue over his glans, then took his cock into her mouth, sucking hard, two fingers masturbating its base, the other hand squeezing his scrotum. For a while he was content to lie unmoving on his back in the near dark, savouring the exquisite sensations Queenie's mouth and hands were bringing him. Then, as she continued to perform down there with her usual unbridled enthusiasm, the feel of a

71

cock in her mouth, the sure knowledge of what this was doing to him causing her pleasure in itself, he reached for her hips, pulled her knickers down her thighs and, hand sliding over her buttocks, found her damp pussy from behind and slipped two fingers inside, up to the third knuckles.

Queenie wriggles her bottom and grunts into the cock. She treats it to one final, voracious suck, unmouths it, trails her tongue along the eight and three-quarter inches from root to glans, then, with Jamie's fingers working deep inside her, kicks off her knickers, moves her lips to his ear and whispers, 'I'm going to fuck you, 007.'

'A feller's supposed to do that to a sheila.' She can just make out his half-smile.

'But I'm a lady, remember? Ladies are privileged.' She straddles him, head bumping the boards of the bunk above, reaches between his thighs, finds his penis, guides it, sinks down all the way on it, and begins to slowly but eagerly ride it as his fingers undo her blouse and her breasts fall free, swinging gently to her rhythm until he takes one in each hand and begins to roll them together.

She can feel a climax building within her – an urgency in him. This, she knows, is to be no marathon screw, but the sensations are everything they should be, uncluttered, uncomplicated by – and without the thorough dissoluteness of – the threesomes and moresomes in which she has so often been involved. As they approach orgasm he tips her sideways, going with her, contriving to keep his penis inside her while he rolls her on to her back. Raising her stockinged feet she crosses them on his heavy buttocks, just above the only slightly lowered jeans, her fingers clawing into the backs of his shoulders, which are beginning to sweat through his shirt, her mouth flattened on his cheek. Her back is pressed into part of the mattress which rests on a slightly loose board; it begins to creak along with his massive thrusts, but both are too far gone in their passion to care about this giveaway. His buttocks and thighs go rigid, his semen pours into her, and she comes along with him, both of them managing to restrain the need for verbal expression. They are still. A minute or so later her eyes flicker open on an upside-down yellow face which peers through the curtains from the bed above, hooded eyes unblinking, unreadable.

Queenie smiles languidly at it. It vanishes. The curtain drops closed.

On their way out, Jamie ventured a couple of questions in Chinese to the custodian, about Masters and Li – questions which were greeted with a stony, suspicious silence. He didn't push the matter.

'There's something very rumpled about you two,' commented Coco as, almost an hour after leaving her, Jamie and Queenie reappeared.

'Is there now?' responded Queenie archly, smoothing her skirt.

'So what did you discover?'

'Ah, it is an opium den,' said Queenie, sitting down. 'Apart from that, nothing at all.'

'Then, what kept you?'

Jamie said, 'They have these ... these sort of cubicles with bunks in, where people settle down to take their opium.'

'I know, I've seen them before.' Her eyes went very wide. 'Jesus, you weren't smoking, were you, Queenie?'

Queenie pursed her lips. 'Not in the way you mean.'

Coco's mouth dropped open. 'You popped into a cubicle? Together? You ...?'

'It was kind of a tight squeeze,' Jamie grinned.

'You let me sit here all this time while you were ... at it?' She gaped at them. 'You rotten bastards!'

'It was jolly nice,' commented Queenie, in her most exaggerated British accent. 'Wasn't it, James?'

# 5

# Whipped? – Cream!

In the briefest of bikinis, Coco lounged by the side of the
ship's small pool, lazily watching the coastline of Taiwan
slide by as the *Star of Kowloon* headed south. It was a
sublime day, the deep blue sky cloudless except for little
puffs clinging to the distant central mountains of the
500-kilometre-long island; the sun was hot, but its bite was
tempered by the ship's own breeze.

'Day's work done?' asked Queenie as she parked her
behind on a sunchair next to Coco, pulling the knot in her
blouse tighter under her breasts.

'Couldn't resist this. Besides, I've shot several rolls of film.'

Queenie turned her face up to the sun and closed her
eyes. 'We are now in the Pacific Ocean,' she remarked. 'In
no time at all, we've come from the South China Sea
through the East China Sea to the Pacific. Amazing.'

'Only little bits of them,' said Coco. 'And in a few hours'
time we'll be back in the South China Sea on our way to
the Philippines. And I don't feel the least tired!' She
glanced at her friend, whose mini skirt was almost as
revealing as her own bikini. 'Get anything worthwhile this
morning?'

Queenie nodded and opened her eyes. 'An interesting
interview with an oil-rich Texan who spends half his life
on trips like this and touring the world's casinos. There's
hardly a casino anywhere he hasn't left money in. Looking

beyond his rather simplistic statements about living for the thrills of gambling, I'd say he's got that strange sickness I came across yesterday – a compulsion to lose. Three-quarters of his annual net income, which he casually refers to as just a few million dollars, goes across the tables. Extraordinary!'

'Will he let me take some pictures?'

'You bet. Dead keen to see himself and his jewellery-dripping missus splashed over a glossy.' She paused. 'I managed to get in a few words with the spying lady of yesterday. When I mentioned we'd noticed her in Taipei she seemed a bit startled, and changed the subject. And by the way, interesting. She's lessy without a doubt. Fancied me madly. German. Very cool, sort of a Garbo type with a marvellously husky voice. Her name's Helga.'

Coco absent-mindedly twisted her long black hair into a thick rope, and draped this over one shoulder as she said, 'And does Helga do anything for a living apart from playing Mata Hari?'

'She said something vague about fashion. But I happen to know my fashion names very well, and hers doesn't fit anywhere in the top league; neither does her face. And following creeps like Masters and Li down Chinese back alleys hardly fits with dress designing.'

'We must get to know her a little better.'

Queenie raised an eyebrow. 'I plan to get to know her a lot better!'

'I might have guessed. I wouldn't mind either.'

'Want to share her? That sounds ... fun. Okay, we've arranged to have a drink together at the cocktail hour. Why don't you show up?'

'Will do. If only to stop her from eating you alive. She looks rather aggressive to me.'

'As long as it doesn't go beyond the playful, that's fine by me.'

Coco grinned at her. 'Hoping for that special excitement? Fancy a touch of the English vice, do you, my lady?'

'I can't think what you could possibly mean. Besides, she's German.'

'And therefore probably good at administering it. Looking forward to a touch of chastisement, are you? Hoping that Helga's into S and M?' Coco teased.

'You're being utterly ridiculous!' But there was a twisted smile on Queenie's lips, and a pensive look about her eyes. 'I must say, she certainly does seem the type, does she not?' she said.

'It seems, I drink with the most loveliest two womens aboard,' observed Helga as, precisely at seven, Queenie and Coco joined her in the bar. They were dressed to kill – stunning. Coco was at her most daring in a Lanvin outfit by Claude Montana; silver pink, sequined bolero hanging loose over unrestrained breasts, and a mid-calf, iced coral, satin folded skirt with a thick, black patent leather belt. And Queenie wore a lilac silk jacket from Valentino, nipped in at the waist over a mosaic metallic T-shirt with matching miniskirt. Helga, in a white catsuit of the finest leather, spiky, white, low boots, and with her blonde hair cascading over her shoulders, was kinkily regal. Green eye shadow complemented her big, emerald eyes, and mauvish make-up accentuated the Slavic cheekbones.

Just about everyone else on the trip had noticed or had some contact with the three women at one time or another, but so far they had never been seen together. This combination, dressed so sensationally, turned heads fast enough to crick necks. And the ladies knew that as surely as each was perfectly aware of her own sexuality, and the direction it was likely to lead to this night.

'So, you were seeing me in Taipei yesterday,' Helga surprised Queenie by saying. 'I was shopping. But how is it I see you not on the bus?'

'We were extravagant. We took a car,' said Coco.

Queenie would very much like to have questioned Helga further about her 'shopping' trip, but thought better of it. Instead she said, 'Do you go on gambling boats often?'

'This is my first time.'

'How do you like it?'

'Is good. I play only little stakes. Some I win, some I

lose.' She shrugged. 'I am doing not so bad. But you two, you are making an article, is it not so? Do you not play the tables therefore?'

'Just a bit,' said Coco. 'Mainly we watch.'

'This is requiring discipline, no?' An intense stare accompanied the words, making Coco almost nervous. 'This article – you ask people many questions, is it not so?'

'Only about their gambling. What motivates them and so forth.'

'It is better so.' Helga fitted a cigarette into a gold holder as she spoke. It came from a sky-blue pack, and was slender, a brand with the name of American Spirit, which neither Coco nor Queenie had seen before. 'You will discover that there are people on this ship who are not liking to be asked many questions.'

'We noticed.' Queenie watched closely for reaction to her next words. 'There's an Englishman called Masters who's very touchy.'

'Oh, really?' The words were accompanied by a slight twitch at the corner of her vermilion-painted mouth. Tiny, but enough. She changed the subject, raising a small, gold Dupont lighter to the cigarette. 'I notice you look at my cigarettes. They are truly the designer cigarettes, very fine, very expensive, with no – 'ow is it you say? Additives? No saltpetre, for example, so they are burning longer.' She lit it, inhaling deeply.

'But plenty of nicotine, I'll bet?' ventured Coco.

'Oh, much. This is for the true smoking aficionado, which I am. It is but one of my several vices.' She smiled disarmingly.

Queenie caught herself behaving like a man, staring longingly at the superbly filled catsuit, imagining what lay beneath it. She dragged her eyes to the German's big green ones. 'Well, gambling is most certainly a vice,' she said. 'What's your favourite game?'

There was a lengthy pause as Helga inhaled luxuriously, letting the smoke trickle from flaring nostrils as she replied, huskily. 'My favourite game of all is the one which I believe we are beginning to play now.' Her eyes drifted sultrily, slowly, from Queenie's to Coco's, and then ran lazily over Coco's Lanvin bolero and the swell of her half-revealed breasts, unspoken sexual intimation in them. '*N'est-ce-pas?*' Then the eyes, having achieved their job of titillation remarkably well, roved vaguely around the bar as she added, 'But if you are talking of gambling, then I will tell you I am liking best the crap dice. It is so full of ... excitement.'

'You enjoy excitement?' asked Queenie, sexual tension building in her belly.

The German's hand, long slender talonous nails painted green to match her eye-shadow, fell on Queenie's white-stockinged knee. 'But of course, my darlink, I am thriving on excitement. Of many different kinds – we are perhaps understanding one another?' The hand gently squeezed.

Boy, are you fast, thought Queenie, pulse racing. 'I am understanding you, yes,' she said, with a crooked little smile.

'You two are perhaps the lovers?' Helga asked, totally matter-of-factly, removing her hand from Queenie's knee after another little squeeze.

'Sure,' said Coco easily, comfortable with this leading question which coming from most other strangers might have needled her. She was as turned on by this enigmatic beauty, as she could sense Queenie was.

'But, perhaps it is that you are not ... exclusive to one another, is this so?'

'No,' said Queenie. 'That is, yes; that's right.'

'Ah. This is very good. I like. Then perhaps, later ...?' The half-smoked cigarette and holder were most carefully laid across an ashtray. One hand found Queenie's knee again, the other lightly gripped Coco's sequin-sleeved forearm. 'No?'

'Perhaps,' said Coco, trying to keep her voice level.

'Excellent.' Suddenly Helga's blatant sexual innuendo vanished. She became brisk, as if she had just settled a straightforward business arrangement, removing her hands, picking up her cigarette holder, puffing briskly. 'Then we should finish our drinks here, have dinner together, get maybe a little light in the department of the head – this is always welcomed, no? – and then we shall see, no?'

Throughout a meal whose conversation was punctuated with libidinous remarks and looks and with over-friendly touching, Queenie tried several times to turn the conversation to Helga's fashion connection but, each time she did, Helga skilfully changed the subject. By dinner's end Queenie and Coco were as wise about what, if anything, the German did for a living as they had been before it.

The three of them got a bit light-headed. Helga managed to polish off two Martell brandies with her coffee before she proposed, in her sexiest voice, that they should go to her cabin for a nightcap.

'Tell you what – we have a suite. Very large and comfortable. Shall we go there?' asked Queenie.

'You have a suite? Is that not tremendous expensive for journalists?'

'Sure is. But happily for us our very good friend owns the boat.' Coco nodded towards a nearby table. 'Jamie Bond.'

Helga followed her gaze. 'Yes, of course, I know him. Very handsome. He is your very good friend, you say. Then perhaps you . . .?'

'Yes,' said Queenie heavily.

'The . . . three of you?'

'Yes,' said Coco.

'You must be exceptionally healthy girls. I like more and more.' She pushed herself to her slightly wobbly feet. 'But let us go to my cabin, no? I am having some interesting toys for us to have enjoyment with.'

'Toys?' whispered Queenie to Helga's back as she walked away with a slight lurch, and as if there could be no question about them following her.

'S and M – what did I tell you?' said Coco, rising. 'Well, she'd better not get beyond the playful.'

'What if she does?' Queenie still had not left her chair. Helga, stopped, was turning around, her hands on her hips.

'Come on, nut.' Coco grinned fleetingly. 'If she starts getting rough I'll tie her in a knot.'

Queenie grinned back. 'True. I was completely forgetting your aikido. In that case . . .' Queenie got to her feet.

'Pull the other one, doll. My aikido or not, a goddamm army couldn't keep you away from her!'

Once they were in her cabin, Helga locked the door behind them, switched on the ship's piped music system and made a production out of unscrewing several light bulbs, before getting herself another brandy and opening a bottle of white wine. She behaved exactly as a man setting his seduction scene. Through the portholes the distant lights of Chialoshui, on the southern tip of Taiwan, slid slowly by; the sea was almost unnaturally still.

'Then, we drink to us,' drawled Helga, handing the girls a glass of cold wine each, clinking glasses with them and downing half the brandy. 'And the evening still to come, no?' Her eye narrowed as it fell on Coco's open-fronted top; on one side the edge of the bolero was almost at her nipple, the whole of the curve of her breast exposed. Helga's free hand reached, slid inside the jacket, caressed. 'You are having the most delightful tits,' she murmured.

Helga's hand felt warm and soft on Coco's flesh, gentle in itself, but her finger and thumb pinched the nipple just enough to cause the slightest twinge of pain. Coco flinched, shivered, closed her eyes briefly, then opened them very wide as the German's lips clashed with hers, mashing them, and her white leather-clad thigh crushed folded satin as she insinuated it tight and hard between Coco's legs.

Queenie stood back a pace, eyes glued to every move as the two – Helga a head taller than Coco – embraced, both wine and brandy splashing to the carpet. She was amused, she was aroused, but she was also somewhat confused as to how this evening was meant to develop; a lesbian threesome was as new to her as she was sure it was to Coco. The suggestion of a little sado-masochism thrown in daunted her.

Responding to Helga's rough advances with great enthusiasm, Coco pressed her crotch on to the rubbing thigh, wriggling her hips as their tongues meshed, and grunting into Helga's mouth, while her stiff nipple was rolled and twisted. After a while Helga pushed her away, holding her at arm's length, breathing heavily while admiring and lusting. '*Schön, sehr schön*,' she muttered. 'But at the same time I must not neglect darling Queenie, is it not so?'

Weakly downing her wine, and leaning back by the side of a porthole, Coco watched Helga advance on Queenie, who sort of flopped into her arms as if she had made up her mind that she was the German's to do with as she pleased. Crotch met crotch, Helga bending slightly at the knees and easing Queenie's metallic miniskirt up on to her hips, so that the only barrier to Queenie's pussy was her white tights and knickers. Her lips drawing on the flesh of Queenie's neck in a love bite, Helga rubbed pussies sensuously with her as her free hand stole down the back of her knickers and rummaged amongst her buttocks. Slightly alarmed at the love bite which was being produced on her neck, Queenie lacked the will to do anything to stop it, so overpoweringly lustful was Helga's sexual attack. Then, as she had done with Coco, Helga broke off her embrace suddenly to hold Queenie at arm's length. 'You, too, are a prize, my darlink,' she intoned. 'I am having, on this night, the most incredible luck of my life.' Taking Queenie by the hand she led her the few steps over to Coco, and put her brandy glass down on a table. Cupping Coco's elbow she moved the three of them to the bed. 'Come,' she murmured, 'we will lie down together and practise things which delight, no? Then, later, perhaps my toys?'

It was a narrowish bed on which three could just fit cuddled up; the danger of one rolling off was confined to one edge only, since the other was tight against the bulkhead. Getting into the middle, on her back, Helga pulled the two girls close into either side of her, her arms wrapped around them, and began kissing first one, then the other. Both had a thigh over hers; her legs were parted and their knees met between them. As Helga indulged in a lengthy kiss with Coco, drawing her tongue into her mouth and sucking on it like a little cock, Queenie slid open the zipper which went from neck to navel of Helga's catsuit, uncovering large breasts encased in a thin, black rubber bra with a big hole in each cup through which protruded erect, rouged nipples. Ducking her head she darted her tongue over one as her hand slipped into the belly of the suit to encounter still more rubber. As she explored lower, above the rubber, she was aware that Helga's hand was once more in the back of her knickers, fingers seeking her vagina from behind, then finding it.

Helga, lips greedily savouring Coco's, squirmed in the triple delight of having Queenie's fingers discover her thick, springy, panty-less bush as she, palms nestling between two pairs of buttocks, began to probe both their pussies at the same time.

The lesbian threesome began to writhe and moan, Helga being its pleasure-centre. As she switched lips from Coco's to Queenie's, Coco's nimble fingers found their way, also, into her pussy, the backs of them tightly worming their way against Queenie's. Suddenly Helga's thigh muscles clamped tight on both their hands, the small of her back arched slightly from the bed, she groaned deeply and huskily twice into Queenie's mouth, then relaxed, breaking the kiss. 'I come,' she moaned. 'Never do I come so quickly!' Her hands went limp in the backs of the girls' knickers; she let loose a long sigh of contentment.

'Me, I'm getting out of my gear,' said Coco, rolling her feet to the floor, and standing up. 'Before it gets totally ruined.' Helga's hand, freed from her knickers, flopped on its back on the bed.

'Me too,' agreed Queenie, easing herself down the edge of the bed against the bulkhead. Sitting on its bottom end, she stripped off the already badly creased Valentino jacket and the metallic T-shirt beneath it, then stood and draped them carefully over a chair, before stepping out of the miniskirt.

Helga watched them with lazy, prurient interest as they speedily got naked. 'What perfect bodies you are having, you two!' she exclaimed when they were nude. She also got to her feet and wriggled out of her catsuit, kicking off her boots to get it over her feet. The black rubber at her waist was a corset whose purpose was certainly not to restrain any excess belly fat. It curved down into suspenders on either side of her buttocks and her pubic mound, provocatively framing them. The stockings were black, with seams decorated from top to bottom with silver, diamond-shaped embroidery. She turned all the way around for them, twice, exhibiting herself with a sultry, artless smile. 'But me, for you, I keep something on. Is nice, no?'

Queenie, her sexual needs highly aroused by the petting, the fingering, further keyed up by the sight of the kinkily encased, statuesque body of Helga, took Coco by the shoulders, bore her on to her back on the bed, and fell on her, kissing her breasts as Coco's fingers found her pussy.

'No, you may not have one another to yourselves!' Helga exclaimed sternly. 'This, you can be doing any night.' Going to a drawer, with a flourish she produced from it a pink rubber dildo, an extraordinary thing, as big as Jamie Bond's erect penis, and incredibly detailed as to the thick vein down its back and the perfectly realistic glans. Attaching it between her legs with a set of velvet straps, then holding it lovingly as if it were the real thing, she approached the bed. As Queenie and Coco, suddenly motionless in one another's arms, watched her with incredulous eyes, she stood above them, saying, 'You have one very good word in English, one word better I think than all others in any language. This work is "fuck". I am loving the German version almost, but not quite as much. Is "*fick*". Now Helga is going to fuck-fick you both in turn. I am very good at it, you shall see. First please, Queenie. Please to kneel on the floor. Lean on the bed.'

This was Helga's show. Thus far Queenie was lapping it up, and her pussy was dying for penetration, any sort of penetration. As she rolled from the bed and bent her knees to the carpet, Helga said, 'Here. Hold this cock a moment. Is like real.'

It surely was. It gave slightly to the touch, it felt smooth, warm even. It had rubber balls, and Helga's thick, black bush overlapping the top of its base made it appear unbelievably lifelike. 'Is my very own cock,' said Helga excitedly as Queenie handled it in wonder. 'Rub it.'

'Rub it?'

'*Ja.* Like when wanking a man.'

Puzzled, Queenie obliged, eliciting a little grunt of pleasure from Helga. 'Is enough,' the German said. 'Just to show you. Behind there is a thing which sheathes my clit, no, and an extension fits up inside me? You wank it, I feel it. I fuck you like a man, I feel it. *Gott* in heaven I feel it!' Her green eyes flashed lust. 'Now, please to bend over the bed. You like to eat Coco's pussy while I do you – then eat!'

'Yeah. You do that!' exclaimed Coco, spreading her thighs around Queenie's face as she positioned herself for it, her toes on the carpet.

Queenie's chin was on the bedspread close to Coco's crotch. She touched her girlfriend's bush with her tongue, sliding her eyes up over Coco's dangling breasts to her face as she murmured, 'This is brilliant!'

It felt exactly like a cock as Helga, on her knees behind Queenie, rammed the dildo deep inside her with one powerful thrust of her hips, and began to tantalise her with short, fast pelvic jerks, while Coco, with Queenie's shoulders flattening her upper thighs and fingers spread on either side of her buttocks, lifted her bottom to make it easier for Queenie's questing tongue to find its way to her clitoris and vagina beyond.

It felt exactly like a cock, and Helga screwed just like a man, getting quickly into a heaving, plunging rhythm, her rubber-surrounded, rouged nipples bouncing on Queenie's back, her tongue finding an ear and probing as her hands rifled Queenie's tits. In and out she jerked, faster and faster, no let-up, panting away, bringing Queenie, mightily aroused, so rapidly towards orgasm that she could no longer concentrate on pussy eating. She pressed her face into the soft inside of Coco's thigh, eyes closed, kissing the hot flesh. As an amazing climax began to rage through her, she was unable to stop her teeth from nipping into Coco's flesh, causing a squeak of pain which was drowned by her own trembling moan.

Helga uncoupled from her, her emerald eyes now gleaming with the light of an almost mad excitement. She looked as if she were about to spit as she snarled, 'You see, like a man I fuck, like a pig man who cannot control himself for to give the womans pleasure. But I know how to do it better than a man. Is this not so? Is it not so?'

In a state of collapse between Coco's thighs, Queenie, drained by the violently exquisite lesbian sex, said nothing. But Coco, leaning back on her hands, the nip of her thigh almost forgotten, a tiny speck of blood, the same colour as its neighbouring tattooed rose, congealing, muttered, 'It sure is, honey. It sure is so!' She gazed in prurient fascination at the German who, on her knees and slightly hunched over, had been furiously masturbating the dildo as if it really were a penis, and now stopped, her hand clutching it, pointing it up at Coco.

'On your back, *mein Schatz.*' The words tumbled from Helga's vermilion lips like hot rocks. 'I tell you, I make you come in less than one minute, and such a coming you will get!'

With open arms and open legs Coco welcomed the luscious lesbian, relishing the challenge since she was already in an enormous state of arousal. The dildo slipped easily inside her and up into her wetness. She brought her legs high, dropping the heels on to the small of Helga's back, and gripped the big, tight, plunging buttocks with both hands. With her weight resting on arms spread on either side of Coco's shoulders, Helga arched her back down to position her protruding nipples so as to touch Coco's, rubbing against them, a raunchy nipple-to-nipple caress, as she gritted her teeth, perspiration breaking out in tiny beads over her forehead and upper lip, while her hips – hips of a grotesquely beautiful transvestite about to climax – bucked and heaved.

Coco moaned quietly, constantly, throughout the entire event, with each and every thrust, rocking her pelvis and feverishly clutching the plunging buttocks, her nails digging in them, raking them, her heels drumming on Helga's back as her vaginal juices seeped over the plastic penis.

Helga shouted something in German, along with Coco's climax, and sank down on to her, tits flattening against tits, dildo rammed deep inside her, mouth buried in her neck. For long, long moments, as she came gradually down from her ecstatic high, Coco was unaware that the dead-weight of Helga was squashing the breath from her. Dragging in a lungful of air, she heaved upwards at Helga's ribs and rolled her off herself on to her back, as the dildo flopped out of her and then – its greatest difference from the real thing, apart from a lack of semen – stayed at attention. For a while Coco lay panting at her side. When she opened her eyes it was to Queenie's amused stare, her head on her hands on the edge of the bed as she sat on the floor. 'All right, was it?' said Queenie.

Coco smiled. 'You should know.' She glanced at Helga, who was staring blankly at the ceiling. 'That's one hell of a dick,' she said.

Helga turned her head to look at her. She was the picture of contented lust; her lipstick and make-up were smeared, her eyes and mouth drooped. Taking hold of the dildo in her fist, she rubbed it gently and muttered, 'Better than the real thing, no? Never it goes down. No bastard man on the end of it, neither!'

'You don't like men one bit, do you?' remarked Queenie, recovered from her orgasm, thoroughly amused.

Unexpectedly, Helga retorted, 'No, I like not the men. They are, they are ... clumsies. But, yes, I take them to my bed – this I cannot help, no?'

'Strokes for folks,' muttered Coco.

'Eh?'

'Nothing. It means it's odd. You refer to them as pigs, but then you let them make love to you.'

'Oh, *ja*, sure. A man in the bed is sometimes very goot.' She grinned. 'But me, I fuck better!'

Neither of the girls chose to disagree. Queenie stood up, stretched, yawned and moved towards the chair where her clothes were draped. 'I guess I'll get dressed,' she said.

'Dressed – not!' Helga responded with her stern voice.

'I don't know. I'm . . .'

'What gives, Queenie?' asked Coco. 'The night, as they say, is young.'

'I simply feel a bit tired. Oh, I feel good, too. That was marvellous, Helga. But I think I need to catch some sleep.'

'But no. This, it is impossible. There is much more to enjoy. Different pleasures of the night. Me, I am expert. You finish the wine; you have more. See.' She swung herself off the bed, unstrapped the dildo and took it to a closet, where she opened a drawer, dropped it inside, and turned around with something shiny in her hand. 'There is this.' Queenie gasped as she let it swing loose: a pair of chrome-plated handcuffs. 'And, there is this.' Reaching behind her, she produced a riding crop.

'Uh – oh. Not quite our scene, sister. Sorry,' exclaimed Coco, the tiniest bit alarmed.

'But I hurt not. I sting a little, this is all. I am bringing only the pleasures. Have we not pain in our pleasure? Look at your thigh, Coco – beside the cute little rose.' Only at that moment aware of its slight smarting, Coco glanced at the little spot of dried blood, now surrounded by a tiny discoloration, where Queenie, in her passion, had nipped her thigh.

Carrying her implements in one hand, Helga went over to Queenie, stretching her other hand to her neck. 'And see this. She liked, I liked.' A nasty-looking small mauve bruise: the perfect example of a love-bite.

Frowning, Queenie found a mirror and examined the mark. 'And I thank you not,' she said drily.

'But you liked. And for many days it is making you remember.' She paused. 'And me, if I am not mistaken. I am marked. *Ja.* Look!' Twisting her torso she gazed down the length of her back, one hand stretching taut the skin of one buttock. There were three long scratches from Coco's nails on it. She examined the other buttock. Two more. 'This, too.' She smiled at Coco. 'You did this, and I like!'

Coco giggled. 'So because of a few scratches and a couple of bites you figure we're ripe for horse-whipping?'

'So silly you are being. I want only to bring pleasure. I sting you a little, on the bottom. We kiss, make up, make love. Is only fun, this you will discover. Now, here.' She put the handcuffs and crop on a table, refilled their wine glasses, then poured a third one for herself. 'Anything you don't like, immediately I stop. At once!'

Queenie looked doubtfully at Coco. But, beneath it all, Queenie, who was game for most everything sexual, Queenie was tempted. She accepted the wine.

Gingerly perching her pleasantly glowing, bare behind on the very edge of the bed, Queenie watched Helga as she fastened Coco's wrists behind her back with the handcuffs which had just vacated her own. Queenie's backside had been on the receiving end of a playful spanking on previous occasions, but nothing so finely tuned, so expertly applied as Helga's administrations with the riding crop. She had proved herself wonderfully familiar with this instrument, more usually applied with some force to the flanks of a reluctant horse, bringing to her short, sharp blows the exact amount of whippiness to produce brief, stinging pains and the pleasure she had so accurately promised. Queenie had not actually climaxed under the tanning, but she had come very close to it, and Helga's mouth had brought her off in seconds when it was over.

'You see my pet,' intoned the German as she snapped closed the links, 'how content is your girlfriend. How she smiles as she wriggles her nicely sore derrière on the bed! For you I bring a similar gratification.'

Coco's eyes dwelt doubtfully on the crop lying on the bed. Her observation of it biting repeatedly into Queenie's buttocks, whilst Queenie knelt on the carpet with one cheek flattened on the bed, had fascinated and excited her. Undoubtedly Queenie had experienced an intense enjoyment from the hiding, but, then, Queenie had a tendency to revel in a bit of friendly corporal punishment. For herself she had never been thrashed. Watching it being done was one thing; being prepared to have it done to herself was quite another. Her buttocks were already cringing, and she found herself struggling slightly against the handcuffs.

'It might be splendid for you both if I beat you while you are kneeling over Queenie's lap,' suggested Helga.

'Oh, yes. Do that!' said Queenie with a smirk.

Coco turned her wrists uncomfortably. 'Perhaps we'd better forget this,' she pleaded.

'But no. You will please consider it a punishment for your earlier behaviour. You have been a very dirty girl. You must be chastised!'

Queenie slapped her waiting thighs encouragingly. 'Get across there, Co. I promise you you're going to love this.'

Coco shrugged weakly in consent, then realised the difficulty; she was obliged to lean into Helga's hands, and so be let down across Queenie's lap. In that position, head and breasts hanging free, knees half bent, toes pressed into the carpet, hands shackled, she felt utterly vulnerable. Buttocks tensed, she waited for the assault.

Helga's expertise lay principally in her wrist. She barely moved her arm at all; there was no need. Carefully she laid the lower nine tapering inches of the flexible, steel-hearted, black-leather-covered crop with its knotted tassel straight across Coco's behind, putting a little pressure on it, so that it curved and indented the flesh. As Coco quivered, she let it rest like that for several seconds, measuring with her eye. Then, with a quick flick of her wrist, she brought the crop up and down sharply through no more than two feet. There was a brief whistle as it cut through the air, followed by a sharp thwack – itself accompanied by an intake of breath and a strangled 'ouch!' as it bit into the buttock flesh in exactly Helga's measured line.

A pause, Coco's toes twitching, teeth biting her lower lip. Helga replaces the crop, making a fresh dent in a line parallel to the first, now clearly defined in red, then repeats the process – whistle, thwack! – as Queenie caresses Coco's neck beneath the tumbling black hair, and this time Coco's feet bounce clear of the carpet, her breasts shudder, and her cuffed hands tremble on her spine. Again, again, again:

five distinct, roughly parallel red welts, which a sixth blow cuts diagonally across. The pauses to measure between each stroke are of exactly the same duration. Helga's rhythm and the strength of her blows are unchanging, and as Coco's behind becomes criss-crossed with those pain/pleasure lines, something amazing happens to her. After the eighth cut, knowing precisely how the ninth will feel and when it will fall, and with the tension dissolved from her buttocks at last – she eagerly awaits it!

The twentieth and final stinging blow. Wet between her legs, her belly churning lasciviously, Coco anticipates the next lash, her backside burning. Nothing happens. Disappointment touches her. Coco the non-believer is panting for more. She hears a movement and, craning her head over her shoulder, she sees that Helga, hands shaky, is fumbling with the straps of the dildo as she impatiently gets it back in place, her needs, after this second administration, overpowering her.

With the thing comfortably in position, she falls to her knees between Coco's thighs. She is a little too low, and needs to pile up two cushions to kneel on before pussy and plastic align. Hands gripping Coco's shoulders she plunges the dildo into her, and once again Helga becomes the rutting male – while Queenie, inflamed by the sight of the beating and now this, slides a hand between Coco's rocking belly and her own thighs, finds her pussy and begins to masturbate.

It is an extraordinary but short-lived sexual event. With its ingenious extensions bringing her rapidly towards orgasm, Helga slams the dildo in and out of Coco, who has been brought – unimaginable earlier – close to climax herself by the thrashing while, hand beneath Coco's belly, Queenie's masturbatory enthusiasm rises to a fury.

In vastly different ways these daughters of Lesbos manage the feat of coming almost in unison in a heaving, gasping, sobbing, climactic explosion. Then all three are still: Helga sagging into Coco's back; Queenie's head and shoulders drooping, her eyes closed; Coco's fingers trailing limp and bent on the carpet.

In a little while, Queenie wriggles uncomfortably, complains about the weight, and Helga, dildo glistening, slips to the floor.

Opening her eyes, Queenie feasted them on Coco's brightly glowing behind, so close to hand. Caressing it, impressed with its heat, she murmured happily, 'Well, isn't that nice. Finally we have exactly matching bottoms, darling!'

# 6

## Hot Coco

. . . Pheewww! – I have enjoyed some magnificently steamy, complicated sexual encounters in my time, as my readers will be aware, but somehow I have never contrived myself into a three-way lesbian swing. How I envy them that one! In case you are thinking that much of what I describe is a product of my somewhat fertile imagination, let me hasten to deny this. Not only did I have Queenie's sketchy but admirable notes to guide me, Coco, one afternoon in my arms here at Stratton, described the experience blow by blow, as it were, in order to bring further excitement to our dalliance. The part concerning the dildo, naturally, prompted me to produce my equally impressive black one, Othello, the star of a couple of Frannie chapters, and I used it on Coco – perhaps not with as much masculine enthusiasm as the enigmatic Helga, but to admirable effect.

But I digress. The *Star of Kowloon*, with at least three of its passengers enshrouded in a certain amount of mystery, sailed slowly on south towards the Philippines, and Manila . . .

'And just how did you come by that?' asked Jamie, as he pulled the collar of Queenie's blue silk blouse to one side to reveal her lurid love bite.

'Shit!' Queenie's fingers jerked to the mark, hiding it. 'I knew I should have put some make-up on that.'

'It wasn't me, was it?'

'No.'

'Coco, then?' His hand left her collar and she pulled it closed.

'None of your damned business.' But as she said this her eyes lingered smilingly on Helga, who was leaning over the rail on the far side of the craps table. Helga looked up and smiled back in response, then pursed her lips and raised a wholly insinuating eyebrow.

'Her?' said Jamie.

'Never you mind, 007.'

'Her.' He studied Helga, who was watching the dice bounce down the table. 'I wouldn't mind having a crack at her myself.'

'She eats men for breakfast.'

'Does she now?'

Helga's big eyes rose sharply to meet his own; it seemed uncannily as if she knew they were talking about her.

As he nodded towards her, Jamie said, 'She can eat me any time!'

Jamie moved on, Queenie with him. Hands behind his back, he was making his regular afternoon's public relations tour of the tables, congratulating winners, soothing losers – the 'usual bullshit', as he termed it.

They approached the fan-tan table, where both Masters and Li were gambling for high stakes. Luk, at Master's shoulder, was in animated conversation with Coco. As Queenie and Jamie passed behind Coco and Luk, Coco's hand stole to the Chinese girl's narrow waist.

'What's she up to?' asked Jamie. 'Getting off with Master's Hong Kong toy?'

'That's already history.'

Jamie stopped them in their tracks. 'You've gotta be kidding. Does Masters know about it?'

'He was there.'

The squarish Australian jaw fell open. 'Jeeesus. That slob? This takes the bloody biscuit! How in hell could she?'

'Needs must when the devil drives,' said Queenie.

'Eh?'

'The devil. There's a soupçon of Old Nick in both of us. I suppose it's one of the things that first attracted us to each other. Something to do with our thorough absorption in good, healthy sex.'

'Are you two intending to go through the whole flaming ship, then? Lay the lot of them?'

Except for a wholly innocent smile, she ignored that. 'We both have a different bit of Beelzebub in us. Personally, I couldn't abide having someone like Masters lay even one finger on me. But my Coco's extremely versatile. She loathes Masters, but the lure of Luk was too strong.'

'Together, you must constitute two of the most incredible chicks walking this earth!'

'Don't be silly. We both have extremely active libidos, that's all.' She changed the subject. 'I'd like to know a bit more about this ship. For the record. What goes on down below, for instance?'

'You want to see the engine room?'

'Please.'

Coco, meanwhile, was attemping to wheedle information out of Luk. Whilst watching Masters lose three thousand Hong Kong dollars without so much as the twitch of an eyelid, she asked, 'Just where does friend Masters get all his loot?'

'I don't know, doll.' Luk smiled disarmingly into her eyes.

'Don't you ever ask?'

Smirking, Luk said, 'Listen, kid. Me, I'm a good-time sheila. When a chick like me finds her bread buttered on both sides, she don't go sticking her nose into the butter factory.'

Coco laughed. 'Well, that's one hell of an original way of stating your case, I guess.' She cocked her head. 'You don't have the slightest clue?'

'Nope. And I don't give a stuffed kangaroo!'

'You're being amazingly colourful today.' Coco squeezed her waist and pressed the side of her thigh into hers.

'I am?' Luk returned the thigh pressure, and covered Coco's hand on her waist with her own.

A familiar, welcome tension seized Coco. 'You wouldn't by any chance feel like . . .?' she ventured.

Luk pursed her lips. 'I was beginning to get bored. And he ain't going nowhere for at least a coupla hours.' She produced a happy, suggestive grin. 'What're we waiting for? Let's go to it, honey!'

As, several minutes later, Coco and Luk, hand in hand, made their way through the door of Masters' cabin, Jamie led the way down an iron ladder into the engine room. As he descended he was looking up, raunchily savouring the view up Queenie's short black skirt, ogling her bare thighs and the tight strip of white knickers cosseting her crotch.

The massive collection of machinery, throbbing and humming away with a life of its own, was impressively immaculate. 'Thirty-four years old,' said Jamie with justifiable pride, resting his hand on a shining chrome guardrail. 'This old tub of mine was gun-running during the Vietnam war – and just look at the condition of those engines today!'

Queenie was suitably impressed, whilst understanding nothing of what she was seeing except the cleanliness. 'Beautiful,' she said, then added, 'How come there's nobody here looking after them?'

'He won't be too far away.'

'He? You mean there's only one?'

'You only need one if you're lucky enough to have a hard-working genius like Bobo in your crew. He tends all this stuff as if it's his own, personal baby.' He nodded towards a massive steel door with rounded corners. 'He's probably through there, in the dynamo room.'

And that's where they found one of the most impressive figures of black manhood that Queenie had ever clapped her prurient eyes upon. The chief engineer – the only engineer – known as Bobo because his actual name was a magnificent tongue-twister, stood an inch taller than his boss. He was wearing greasy sneakers and cut-off jeans. He had on no shirt and his massive, coal-black chest gleamed perspiration, accentuating rippling muscle. Around thirty years old, he had a toughly expressive face with negroid lips but a contradictory, thinnish, almost Roman nose.

Queenie, the quintessential adorer of male beauty and raw power, was mightily impressed. The effect on her of being introduced to this man was much the same as that upon a red-blooded young stud when meeting some topless Brooke Shields; her libido took instant command of a head gone suddenly flaky.

Bobo answered Queenie's almost breathless questions with studied politeness, speaking in a resonant voice whose accent she was unable to place. Yet there seemed to be a certain challenging insolence in the way he stared at her as he did so, as if he was perfectly aware of the effect his physical presence was having.

Jamie seemed unaware of the subtle change in her as he continued with the guided below-deck tour. She now paid only cursory attention to the things he pointed out to her, or what he was saying. The image of those gleaming black muscles and Bobo's white-toothed, engaging, and suggestive smile stayed with her, casting its spell. When Queenie and Jamie finally parted, in the casino once more, Queenie, her stomach a tense knot, almost alarmed at her own daring but unable to stop herself, made her hesitant way right back down to the heart of the ship – to the engine room.

By the time Queenie was pushing open the cream, steel bulkhead door with the words NO ENTRY – CREW ONLY painted on it in red, Coco and Luk meanwhile were naked and wrapped in each other's arms on Masters' bed. As they kissed, the *Star of Kowloon* – which had been steaming for more than twenty-four hours in perfectly calm water – began a long, slow roll to starboard, as she met the beginning of turbulence.

Queenie encountered no one on her journey through the crew's quarters. As she picked her way carefully down the steel rungs of the ladder and into the engine room, Bobo, wiping his hands on an oily rag, leant his weight back on a protection rail, his eyes glued on her descending bare legs betraying the keenest of sexual interest.

'Oh. Uh, hello again,' she said with a brightness she did not feel, as, on reaching the steel deck, she turned around to face Bobo, her hands still resting on the sides of the ladder.

'Hi there.' He continued to clean his hands, taking special care of the nails, as his dark eyes ran frankly up and down her body. Apart from her short skirt she wore snowy white Reebok training shoes, rolled-over pink ankle socks, and a tight, eggshell blue, short-sleeved blouse. 'Lost your way, have you?' he asked. 'Or were you looking for something in particular?'

Realising that she had found her way back down there in the mists of something bordering on a daydream, and that she had considered no plan or excuse, Queenie – unusually for her – stumbled over her words. 'I, I'm a repor . . . a journalist,' she said.

'I know it. Mister Bond, he made that clear.'

'Well, it's just that Jamie, Mister Bond, kind of whisked me very fast through here.' The ship suddenly rolled heavily to port. Queenie had been moving away from the ladder towards Bobo, and she tottered and grabbed the protection rail for support. 'I have some questions for you.'

He flashed his white teeth at her. 'Fire away, lady.'

'Yes. Yes.' Her eyes dwelt briefly on his pectoral muscles then watched her own hand as she moved nearer to him, keeping tight hold of the rail as the boat began a long, creaking roll back to starboard. She was finding his close physical presence almost overwhelming. 'What, um, where do you come from?' she asked.

Leaning in the same spot against the rail, comfortably riding the *Star of Kowloon*'s long roll as he stuffed the rag back in his pocket, he watched her in amusement as she fished a notepad, with pencil attached, from where it was hooked over her belt. She then let go of the rail, pencil poised, as the ship stilled. 'Well?' she said.

'I'm one of those impossibly freaky combinations.' He laughed shortly. 'I'm half Zulu and half American Indian.'

'Zulu? Really? Indian?' She gaped at the man, jotting nothing in her notepad. 'How extraordinary.' She was staring at him in almost rapturous admiration, considering her next move – when the South China Sea arranged for her what she was longing to contrive herself. The sideways swell met a frontal wave, and the ship was awkwardly tipped from prow to stern. Dropping her notepad, Queenie snatched at the rail, missed, and was sent staggering, arms windmilling, into Bobo's barrel chest. Had he not been in the way she would have crashed into the steel bulkhead; as it was, he stopped her as if she were no more than a feather borne on the breeze. Laughing aloud, his arms wrapped around her, holding her close.

'Is this perhaps what you came back for?' he muttered, as the boat began another sideways roll.

Her cheek crushed against the muscular warmth of his upper chest. Heart thumping wildly, she slid her eyes hesitantly up to his. 'Yes,' she confessed, 'I suppose it is.' As his big hands tightened into the small of her back, she planted a kiss on his nipple.

'Engines are goin' to have to look after themselves for a while then, don't they?' A hand dropped to the swell of her buttock.

'Too right,' she hoarsely whispered, taking the nipple between her teeth, and chewing on it. In the region of her tensed belly, digging into it, his penis was stirring within the cut-off jeans.

'Who sent you?' he asked. 'Mister Miracle Maker himself?'

'The devil,' she muttered into his nipple, rocking her belly against his rising hard-on as he kept the two of them in perfect balance. 'He's a bad, bad old man.'

'The devil he is,' he said. 'I'll go for that.' His other hand slid down the inward curve of her spine to reach her buttocks too, then both hands slipped beneath them, fingers clutching and groping as he used his chin on the top of her head to move it away from his chest, and lowered his thick lips to hers.

She had never kissed lips like those before. They were

perhaps the only visual feature of the man which failed to excite her, but once their mouths were joined, his half as large again as hers, she found the lips soft, gentle and amazingly sexy.

The ship went through another uncomfortable prow-to-stern lurch, and even Bobo wobbled somewhat. 'My hidey-hole's through there,' he said, raising his chin to one side. Without waiting for any response from Queenie, he swept her up into his arms. Queenie thrilled to this macho Rhett Butler treatment, as he carried her through into a small, dark cabin, where he dumped her on her feet and bolted the door. 'Grab a hold of that,' he told her, nodding at a steel hook near the single porthole. 'I'll fix up a hammock – the sea's going to cut up mighty rough.' Outside the clouds thickened and the tiny cabin grew gloomier.

Up above in Masters' cabin, Coco and Luk had raised a wooden protector at the side of the bed away from the bulkhead, to prevent them being rolled clean out of it. Like two happy, naughty schoolgirls they caressed, kissed and giggled as the South China Sea flung them from one side to the other, locked together.

'Woweee!' exclaimed Coco, breathlessly, as they were spun through three hundred and sixty degrees, as she arrived where she had started, underneath Luk but her side jammed against the bulkhead. 'This is one hell of a ride!'

'Daddy Neptune's rockin' the boat and we're his naked mermaids,' Luk mumbled, arousing another burst of the giggles from Coco.

Queenie and Bobo, still wearing their clothes, had now made it into the big hammock, which easily adjusted to accommodate the two of them. The problems of staying on her feet whilst Bobo clambered in and then hauled her up beside him had done nothing to dampen Queenie's passion. Now that her body was stretched against his in the swaying hammock, with his unabated hard-on digging into her groin, a flood of carnal desire rushed through her.

'Only way to travel,' said the Zulu Indian. As the cabin

dipped from one side to the other, the hammock remained relatively steady, its ropes creaking. His calloused fingers undid three of the buttons of Queenie's blouse, and his hand slid inside it, completely engulfing one breast.

Queenie's insides were beginning to melt away. Only now in this hole of a cabin, only now in the arms of a total stranger, was she aware that she had brought herself into this situation with barely any coherent thought. It was unreal, wild, a degree of daring she had not realised she was capable of. Deliriously happy at what she had done, she gasped into those fat, mauvish lips as the hand crushed her breast and his other one stole confidently under her skirt and up between her smooth thighs.

The fingers which wormed under the crotch of her knickers and eased its way into her pussy triggered off an irrepressible temptation in her. As it reached the first joint she raised a shoulder from the closely woven webbing, unclipped a press-stud on the top of his shorts, unzipped them and, from beneath underpants which were a startling white in contrast to his ebony flesh, brought forth a penis of commendable proportions – almost as big as that of his boss. At that moment the thrill of holding a strange black cock in her palm, its warmth, its throbbing strength, overpowered the sensations that his plundering hand and penetrating fingers were bringing her.

Freeing her arm from under her, she took hold of the far edge of the hammock, heaving herself into a sitting position. She let go of the penis in order to ease the cut-offs down to his knees, then grabbed Bobo with both hands behind his powerful thighs and pulled her head all the way down until her mouth closed over his glans.

Bobo flares his aquiline nostrils, heaves his hips and grunts. His hand drops away from Queenie's breast and creeps over the collar of her blouse to flatten on her neck beneath the tumbling red tresses, while the finger in her pussy intrudes deeper. Queenie brings him to ecstatic heights with her mouth and her tongue, as he rests his eyes on the knobs of her curving spine which bump their way through her tight blouse, staggered at the unbelievable fortune which has brought this horny beauty to his engine room.

As Queenie sucks on, lustily engrossed in one of her favourite sports, marvelling at how long it has been since she last had a black penis between her lips, Bobo's hands change position and intent. Grasping the hem of her skirt on either side of her thighs, he works it up over her hips to her waist. He eases her knickers down her thighs, then sits up, stooping forward over the head buried in his lap, and gets the knickers all the way down and off over her Reeboks. His big hands wrap themselves around the top of her thighs, gripping hard. He mutters, hoarsely, 'Don't stop, kiddo,' and she finds her lower half being lifted and swung through space. Her mouth swivels on his cock, her breasts slide over his belly, the two remaining closed buttons of her blouse torn open by it, and he lets her crotch down over his face to bury his tongue in her pussy. Queenie is now lying head to toe on top of this unusual product of Zulu and American Indian, in the classic sixty-nine attitude. They eat each other with ravenous enthusiasm.

The rolling and dipping of the *Star of Kowloon* intensifies in a swell which has become far too heavy for the stabilisers to alleviate. Yet the hammock dips only from one end to the other, from prow to stern, with the ship; the port and starboard rolling it rides with a small, comfortable swing, the cabin rocking around it – and its mouth-to-genitals, raunchily contrasting couple, female ivory white flesh and tumbling copper hair draped over the blackest of black male bodies.

Utterly engrossed in what she is doing in this unlikely, dismal setting, Queenie busily treats Bobo's genital area to every trick in her sexual book. As the engineer's tongue probes her pussy, sending waves of pleasure through her loins, while his hands range over her buttocks, pinching and squeezing, she fists his cock and trails the wet tip of her tongue over his heavy, hairy, trembling testicles ... runs the tongue along the short valley between scrotum and anus to lick his bottom hole, lingering there, making him shudder and gasp, then all the way back to the root of his cock, before beginning over again the mightily arousing trick known as 'around the world'.

They soixante-neuf some more, until at last he says, replacing his tongue with two fingers and stretching her labia with them, while ogling her pussy, 'I have this strange, perverted desire to put my cock in there!' When he pronounces the word 'cock', with heavy emphasis, he rams his two fingers all the way up there. She grunts into his hard-on, her mouth leaves it, with regret, for the last time, and once again she finds herself man-handled, swivelled around on his belly to come face-to-face with him. His tongue probes between her lips, finding hers, his hand guides his penis into her vagina, and she begins to ride him wildly, bucking and heaving her hips in furious need as the hammock goes up and down like a see-saw when the cabin isn't rolling around them.

This copulation does not last long; it cannot; it is the totally abandoned, first-time fuck of two people who find they are sexually drawn together as magnet to lodestone. With a roar like a wounded bull elephant, drowning out her squeals, he bangs his hips to meet her climactic, massive downthrust, his buttock-blanketing hands drag her pubis hard into his and he begins to flood inside her, his semen spurting on, and on, and on, his exceptionally long orgasm having the magical effect of prolonging her own.

It is over. His arms flop to his sides, hands slightly clenched, palms upwards. She goes limp as a rag doll on top of him, impaled still, his sperm beginning to trickle out of her as his penis wilts. After long, luxurious minutes, the ship yaws violently, the hammock begins to swing much more than before, and Bobo, at last opening his eyes, pats her bottom and drawls, 'You know something, sugar? We gotta get to know one another better. You can make a start by telling me your name!'

In the casino the games are breaking up. In such unusually rough sea, gambling is severely disrupted. Blackjack and chemin-de-fer shoes are skidding about, possessed of a life of their own, chips running wild. On the fan-tan table the little counters are beyond control, rolling all over the baize with the motion of the boat. Masters heaves himself to his feet and begins a precarious, weaving dance out of the casino.

Not having been indulged in the comfort and safety of a hammock, Coco and Luk's lovemaking has not enjoyed the success of that between Queenie and Bobo, but for a while it had been marvellous fun. It came to an inglorious end when Luk was suddenly overcome with nausea. Holding her belly, the Chinese girl lurched into the bathroom, and Coco seized her opportunity to see what she could discover about the mysterious Masters.

Clutching at anything which would help keep her on her feet, Coco worked her way around the cabin to the wardrobes and began a hasty search of the drawers next to where Masters' clothes were hanging: the usual male paraphernalia, much of it in questionable taste – underpants, shirts, socks, ties. Amongst it, a passport. British, Max Kydd. Profession, company director. Another British passport; the name this time Max Bryant, same profession, same photograph. But as Coco groped in the back of the drawer, and as her hand came into contact with the cold metal of what could only be a gun, the cabin door banged open and Masters himself staggered in. He tottered to the bed, arms windmilling and slumped heavily on it – before he noticed Coco, naked, her hand in his drawer.

'What the bleedin' 'ell are you doin', lady?' he snarled, eyes aflame with outrage.

As she snatched her hand from the drawer, Coco made an admirable effort at controlling her voice. 'Max!' she exclaimed cheerfully. 'Hello – I was just searching for a Kleenex.'

'Sure. Sure you were.' His eyes pigged furiously over her nakedness, which she made a half-hearted attempt to hide with her palms. 'Been 'avin it off with Luk, 'ave you?'

'She's throwing up in the bathroom.'

'That I can believe. But the Kleenex bit, no. What the fuck are you up to, you little whore?'

'Don't you dare call . . .' She stopped in mid-sentence as, the ship in one of its momentary calms, he stood up and came towards her, hands extended menacingly.

'I'll get the fuckin' truth out of you,' he snarled, reaching for her, 'even if I 'ave to break your fuckin' neck!'

His move to the attack brought Masters one of the biggest surprises of his life. Using her aikido knowledge and experience to crippling advantage, Coco went into action, jabbing him in a fierce *atemi* strike with stiffened fingers into the junction of chin and neck. As his hands flew to his throat, she grabbed a wrist, using his own stumbling motion to help hurl him against the bulkhead with a skilful *kotegeishi* throw. Gasping and swearing, Masters doubled up in pain on the floor as Coco began to scramble into her clothes.

Ashen-faced, Luk appeared from the bathroom, supporting herself on the door-frame. As the ship began another roll she stared in amazement at the stricken Masters and then at Coco who, gripping a wardrobe knob with one hand, was pulling on her knickers, her skirt held in place with the other. 'How the bloody hell . . .?' Luk began. 'Why the bloody hell?' she finished.

'Sorry, Luk, he attacked me.' Coco shrugged. 'I was searching for a Kleenex and he came for me. I had to get in first. I break easily.'

Rasping for air through his damaged windpipe, Masters heaved himself to his knees. He was going to be badly bruised, but nothing was broken. As Coco took an erratic course towards the cabin door, he raised his head and hissed, 'I'm gonna kill you for this!'

'First you'd better catch me, hadn't you?' Coco threw over her shoulder, and was gone.

Two decks below her, Queenie and the chief engineer, he now riding on top of her, were once again enthusiastically copulating in the swaying hammock.

# 7

# Come Riding!

The South China Sea ceased its raging as the *Star of Kowloon* began to come abreast of the west coast of Luzon, the largest of the more than seven thousand Philippine Islands. By the time, several hours later, she approached the Gulf of Manila, the waves had flattened out. In the gulf itself there was scarcely a ripple; it was as quiet as a lake on a windless day.

The weather was uncomfortably hot and sticky, both temperature and humidity in the eighties; there was heavy cloud cover but no rain. Finding Queenie leaning alone on the rail near the prow of the ship, studying the slowly enlarging Manila skyline, Jamie propped his elbows on the rail next to her.

'Typhoon threatening,' he said.

'We are getting a bit of weather here and there, aren't we?' Queenie ran a handkerchief over her perspiring brow.

'Time of the year. Doesn't put the gamblers off, though, thank Christ.' He draped an arm over her shoulder. 'Been here before?'

'Once briefly. It brings back unlovely memories. I had my handbag nicked right off my shoulder.'

Jamie granted. 'There's as big a bunch of thieves and con artists in Manila as you'll run across anywhere in the world. If there's one place you shouldn't get into conversation with strangers – especially nice, friendly ones with big, open smiles – this is it.'

'Great city.'

'But the country's fine, once you get out of Manila. That is, except for the pirates if you're island-hopping on a small boat. Wonderful beaches. Got some good horseflesh, too. You ride, Queenie?'

'Me?' she chuckled. 'Born in the saddle, I was. Find me someone from my background who doesn't ride, and you'll find me a wimp.'

'Good. Tell you what.' He turned her to face him. 'Know what I've got a hankering to do with you?'

Looking up into his eyes, her heart missed a beat. A powerful, sexy, black mechanic was one thing, but by no means had her contortions with the virile Bobo diminished her hots for his boss. Smiling, she touched his nose with the tip of her finger. 'Surprise me.'

'We'll do it tomorrow, providing the rain holds off. I'll take you on the ride of your life.'

'You will?' Queenie shivered despite the heat. 'Just what do you mean by that, Mister Bond?'

'You wanted a surprise.'

'Okay. What about Coco, then? She likes to hack out.'

'Her too, sure. She's a game chick.' He squeezed her shoulder and planted a kiss on her cheek. 'Gonna be a bit tiring on poor old Arnold, though!' he said, with a broad grin and a wink. He left her gazing in perplexed astonishment at his departing back.

'Let's hope it doesn't rain, in that case,' she murmured to herself.

There was a dockside commotion shortly after they anchored in Manila harbour. Queenie and Coco, in no hurry to disembark, were in their suite when there came the unmistakable sound of two gunshots from the quay, close to the ship. Through a porthole each they watched as a Filipino crew member, whom they recognised as one of the barmen, apparently uninjured by the bullets, was overpowered and handcuffed by customs police. There was a great deal of shouting and arguing. And much arm-waving going on for no apparent purpose. A white plastic carrier bag, which the man had dropped, was retrieved by a customs man as the barman struggled and protested. From within this the policeman produced a brown paper parcel which he jabbed threateningly under the captive's nose, then offered to a leashed Alsatian dog, who sniffed at it and happily wagged its tail and yelped.

'Drugs, stupid bastard,' commented Queenie.

'Poor bastard, you mean,' said Coco as she shot picture after picture through the porthole. 'He'll get fifteen years at least, possibly the death penalty. They're unbelievably tough here.'

'Hold on just a minute,' exclaimed Queenie. 'Will you feast your eyes on those two!'

Masters and Li, standing on the dock with Luk hovering behind them, some fifty yards away from the incident, were watching it with far more than casual interest. Masters' face betrayed anger; he was clearly arguing with Li. As, still struggling and protesting his innocence, the now presumably ex-barman was led away, and Coco swung her camera to Masters, the Englishman's mouth moved ferociously. He banged the fist of one hand hard into the palm of the other.

'Well, that was unmistakable, if you're only half a lip-reader,' Queenie commented. 'Plainly, our yobbos are upset. "Fuck it," Masters said – and just look at the Chinaman.'

Li was staring after the departing group with an expression of the utmost ferocity. The two men's argument seemed to grow fiercer. They began to gesticulate wildly at one another, while Luk shifted her weight from one foot to the other and said nothing.

'The plot, as I believe George Villiers second Duke of Buckingham said, something like three centuries ago, thickens.' Queenie remarked, smug, as usual, about knowing the source of an aphorism. 'One false passport, at least, if not the both of them. A gun tucked away. Now this.

107

That was a drug bust – and those two fine gentlemen are involved.'

'You think the guy was running for them?'

'That's what it looks like, doesn't it? What else?'

'I should have done Masters more damage when I had the chance. He was on the deck, at my mercy, I could have . . .' Coco stared moodily at the three as they began to walk away from the ship, gratified to notice that Masters was walking with a slight limp. But she failed to elaborate on what injury she might have inflicted on him.

'No you shouldn't.' Queenie turned her back on the porthole. 'You're in trouble enough with the man as it is.'

'I hate those bastard drug people. They cause so much fucking misery in the world. I could have killed him, you know. I know exactly how to kill – you know I do. When he was down it was simply' – she levelled her hand in karate chop fashion – 'that, smartly across the bridge of his nose. Drive a splinter of bone into his brain and kaput!'

Queenie looked at her in alarm. 'And kaput, Coco, too, you idiot, when the police get hold of you. You've never done something like that, and I hope you're never going to.'

'Yeah, you're right.' Coco sighed. 'It's just that I get so mad at bastards like that. And the poor Filipino who probably doesn't know any better, after some extra bread, he gets the chop. And to think that I, with Luk and Masters, I . . .' She shook her head, angry.

'To think that you what?'

'Nothing.'

'So he didn't just watch, then?'

'Never mind, Queenie. Don't try to make me talk about it. It seemed kind of okay at the time. Now it's . . .' she shuddered and changed the subject. 'Tell you what, now we know that those two are definitely connected with the drugs business, it's rather up to you and me to do something about it. Trap the bastards somehow, and get them behind bars.'

'Jesus, darling, we're here to produce an article for *Madame*, remember? It's dead dangerous, what you're suggesting.' She chewed her lip thoughtfully. 'Still, it appeals,' she confessed, 'the idea of seeing them locked up. But I rather enjoy my good health.'

'So do I. But for better or for worse we're kind of in it now, aren't we? Anyway I am.'

'Well.' Queenie was silent for several seconds. Then she said, 'We're forgetting Helga. Where does she stand in this business, I wonder?'

'Search me. The obvious way to find out is simply to ask her.'

'We could try,' agreed Queenie, but doubtfully. Their conversation was interrupted by a sudden unheralded streak of lightning, an enormous clap of thunder on its heels, and everyone on the dockside rushed for cover as rain sheeted out of the oppressive cloud-bank like a solid wall.

Helga was nowhere to be found on the ship; it appeared she must have been one of the first to go ashore. The wind stood up and howled, screaming around the *Star of Kowloon*, which began to rock and strain on its moorings as the harbour waters broke into wavelets. With lightning forking and flashing all over the sky, and thunder booming and rumbling, for more than an hour all hell broke loose. The typhoon vanished as quickly as it had arrived, but rain continued to fall heavily, and the girls elected to give Manila a miss – at least for that night. Each other's arms would be welcome enough entertainment.

The following day dawned dazzlingly sunny. The storm, it seemed, had cleared the air, sweeping much of the humidity away with it. A most cheerful Jamie joined Queenie and Coco for breakfast. 'Looks like a great day for that ride I suggested,' he said through a mouthful of crispy bacon.

'Ride? What ride?' asked Coco.

'I threatened to take Queenie on the greatest ride of her life – and believe me I meant what I said. She volunteered you along, Coco. Er, horses also have something to do with it.'

'Paleface talk with forked tongue,' responded Coco. 'But it sounds smashing anyway.' She looked at him archly. 'Horse riding tends to make you horny.'

'In England we just say riding. The horses are taken for granted,' said Queenie with a satisfied little smile. 'Noel Coward.'

Coco kicked her ankle under the table. 'Do shut up, you idiot!'

'Make me horny, too, Queenie?' asked Jamie, buttering a small piece of toast.

She giggled. 'You bet!'

'Good. Because I've got something very special in mind.'

'I rather gathered that. All this double talk.' Queenie pursed her lips. 'Your funny remark about Arnold yesterday,' she added. 'What was that about, you dirty-minded Aussie, you?'

'You'll both find out soon enough, won't you? I'll give you a clue. Where we're going is such a turn-on in itself, you're not going to believe it. It's quite a way from here, on the other coast. Wide, flat, fantastic deserted beaches. No horses there, no people. But there's a stables outside Manila who know me well. We're going to take three horses in boxes, and all the gear, plus a stable-boy to tack up for us over there.' He paused. 'I bet you don't have riding boots with you, do you?'

'Shit no,' said Queenie.

'I guess it doesn't matter, since we'll be sticking to beaches. Trainers'll do. Wear shorts, if you like.'

Queenie grinned flatly. 'What I reckon,' she said slowly, 'is that you're planning to bonk us on that beach, 007!'

He raised an eyebrow. 'Now, would I dream of such a thing?'

'Of course not.' She cocked her head. 'We'd better take a packed lunch with lots of wine, hadn't we?'

The procession which arrived at the white beach north of Infanta, across from Polillo Island, was nothing if not colourful. The 'horse box' turned out to be an ancient open-topped truck with red, orange and green stripes along its wooden sides, and two chestnut mares and a white stallion crammed together in it. This was preceded by a wildly painted jeepney carrying Jamie and the girls – it was a ubiquitous form of Filipino transport: a reconstructed jeep, one of thousands left behind in the Philippines after World War II by the departing United States Army. It carried a selection of twenty blue, red and white lights on its front, was arrayed with more than a dozen driving mirrors, an assortment of chrome animals including two cockerels and three cows, and was sprayed scarlet, silver and gold. At the slightest excuse the driver would sound one of three tune-playing klaxons, amusing at first but tiresome in the extreme well before the end of the slow, almost two-hour drive.

They unloaded their gear and the horses on a dirt road behind dunes thatched with a coarse grass. Jamie and Queenie helped the stable-boy tack up while Coco, clueless as far as that sort of activity went, climbed a dune and sat on top of it, spellbound by the magnificence of the beach with an aquamarine sea breaking gently on it. By half past twelve the three of them were mounted, and Jamie led them up and over the dunes, sliding down the other side, the horses up to their knees in sand. The beach, with no sign of man or beast on it, stretched as far as the eye could see in both directions, wide and hard from a recently retreated tide.

As they broke into a slow and easy canter, horses' hooves thumping dully on the sand, Queenie said, her long red hair flowing behind her, and eyes sparkling, 'I don't believe this. It's like one of those marvellous west of Ireland beaches, but with sunshine!'

'I know exactly what you mean,' Jamie replied, cantering alongside her. 'The dunes, the colour, the islands out there. But you don't see that terrain in Ireland – though it's just as green.' He nodded inland as they slowed their mounts to a walk. Rice terraces, much the same famed, lush, emerald-green colour of wet Ireland, were piled one upon the other in beautifully undulating steps, a most graceful scenic sculpture going on for mile after mile after mile. He

111

stopped his mare, which was beginning to sweat on the neck and haunches. 'Must be one of the most beautiful places on earth, here.' Stroking the horse's neck, he said, 'Let's take them for a paddle. Cool them off.'

They splashed a bit through the shallows, the horses enjoying it, ears pricked forward, tails flicking. Then Jamie led them back up the gently-sloping beach and reined in. Leaning, one hand on the other on the front of his saddle, gently rocking back and forth, he cast a most sensuous eye over the girls in turn, probing their curves, his stare carrying with it blatant sexuality. They both looked, as always, tempting. Queenie was wearing a tight white blouse and jeans, Coco a blue denim shirt, its collar up, and sexy little white shorts. 'Okay,' he drawled at last with a brief, almost evil grin. 'Who's going to be first?'

'For what, Jamie?' Queenie asked, expecting just about anything except his next words.

'Bet you've never done it on horseback, have you?'

Her mouth dropped open as Coco laughed in appreciation. 'On a horse?' Queenie gasped. 'You must be kidding!'

'A trotting horse!'

'You're totally nuts!' exclaimed Coco.

'Could be. Must have rubbed off from you two. But I have done this before. So,' he grinned again, but his eyes were smouldering, 'who is going to be first?'

'He means it,' said Queenie flatly.

'He means it.'

Queenie still gaped. 'I don't believe this.'

'You'd better. You, then,' he decided. Side-stepping his horse to hers, he took hold of the bridle. 'Off you get, Queenie – and out of your jeans and knickers.'

'You can't be . . .?'

'Absolutely.' She was in the saddle still, blinking at him, eyes wide. 'Move it then, kid. Or hasn't the daring Lady Granville got the balls?' he said.

'O . . . kay.' Very doubtfully, Queenie swung a leg over the horse's neck and launched herself to the sand. At that moment she was feeling totally confused. Apart from being sceptical about the plausibility of making love on horseback, she was faced with the obligation to strip naked from the waist down, with Jamie and Coco sitting placidly on their mounts, ogling her. Strangely, having had sex on two occasions with Jamie and countless ones with Coco, calmly getting out of her knickers on this Filipino beach – and not with swimming in mind – she felt extremely shy.

Painfully aware of the lecherous amusement in Jamie's eyes, she unlaced her Reeboks, took them off with her socks, climbed out of her jeans, and stood doubtfully looking up at Jamie in tiny pink Dior briefs, her short blouse just reaching her navel.

'You heard the man,' said Coco, tauntingly, leaning forward in exaggerated interest, her chin propped on one hand, elbow on her thigh. 'Jeans and knickers, my dear!'

With an irritated little frown at her, Queenie hooked thumbs into the sides of her panties, pulled them down her thighs and quickly stepped out of them. Her bush glinted copper in the sunlight. 'All right, now what?' she ventured, resisting the impulse to hide her pubic area with her hands.

'I guess it's my turn.' Jamie cocked a leg over the saddle and sat sideways, freeing his other foot from the stirrup. The mare stood perfectly passive except for swaying its head and swishing its tail, as Jamie shoved a foot forward. 'Pull my boots off, would you?'

Suddenly aware of the pleasant heat of the sun on her bare backside, beginning to get used to the peculiar set of circumstances in which she found herself, Queenie dragged Jamie's Spanish leather riding boots off, one at a time, while he unbuckled his belt and unzipped his jeans. With his boots lying on the sand he raised his bottom, levering with both hands on front and back of the saddle. 'Now the rest of the gear,' he said.

'My, my. I'm getting quite a show,' commented Coco, as her horse, the stallion, decided to do a little snorting dance. She calmed it down with a few experienced touches on the reins, and with her knees. 'But, hell, I'm forgetting something!' she added. From a hip pocket in her shorts she produced a small, flat Minolta camera. She quickly focused it on Queenie and Jamie, and took a couple of shots as Queenie eased his jeans and underpants down over his knees, and off. She urged her mount in closer with a little touch of her heels and took another shot of Jamie from head to knees as he lowered himself back, sideways, into the saddle, penis at half mast.

Confronted with Jamie in a similar, somewhat lewd state of undress as herself, his naked groin on a level with her face, a foot or so away, Queenie was beginning to experience distinct and welcome libidinal stirrings. Unable to drag her eyes from his formidable cock, last encountered in the bunk in the Taiwan opium den, she watched it grow bigger and more erect in tiny little jerks.

'Will you quit gawping at it and get it up?' exclaimed Jamie.

'You bet!' Leaning forward, Queenie took Jamie's penis at the root with finger and thumb, resting her other hand on the warm, muscular, sweaty flank of the horse. She briefly touched the eye of the cock with the tip of her tongue, then drew it into her mouth.

'Oh, wow, hot stuff!' muttered Coco, shooting off more shots, her pussy beginning to tingle.

Jamie's eight and three-quarter inches were up in less than a minute, by which time Queenie was more than ready for them. 'Now what?' she asked throatily, as she unmouthed him.

He swung himself back into the saddle, facing front, his erection pointing slightly upwards from it and resting over the top of its very low pommel. But he kept his legs hanging straight down, his feet loose on either side of the mare's belly. 'Put your foot in the stirrup as you normally would,' he instructed, 'but the wrong way around. Then climb up to face me.'

Nimbly, Queenie did so, fishing for the other stirrup when she was up, and easily finding it. She was now astride the horse, just in front of the saddle, with Jamie's glans digging into her belly.

'Okay,' said Jamie, smiling crookedly at her, his eyes oozing sex. 'This is only possible on an English-style saddle. Anything like a Spanish one or a cowboy saddle with a big pommel is no good.' He found her bush with two fingers, then slid them beneath it, knuckles against the horse's hairy spine, hooking the fingertips into her fractionally, finding warm dampness. 'Ready?'

'No!'

'Let's do it, baby.' Jamie got a grip of his cock near the base and lifted it skywards, pointing it towards her covered breasts. 'Stand up and get yourself over it.'

Queenie's face drooped with amused lust. Hands on his shoulders for balance she stood on the stirrups and rocked forward, positioning herself for impaling. He guided his glans beneath her red bush, found her labia with it, and she lowered herself on to his erection, sinking more than half of it into her pussy before the slope of the saddle made further penetration impossible. 'Oo, oo, ooo!' she moaned, through clenched teeth, shivering in delight, gazing down at this singular coupling.

'Fuckin' hell!' exclaimed Coco, still shooting pictures.

Jamie, his forearms resting on either side of Queenie's bare thighs, took a confident grip on the reins. 'The idea is to let the horse do the work,' he said. 'We trot. I sit in. Since you have the stirrups, you post trot – on Arnold!'

'This is just the most incredible . . .' murmured Queenie, instinctively rocking her hips.

'I said, let the horse do the work! Let's go!' He flicked the reins, drummed his bare heels into the mare's belly, and they broke into a steady trot, an excited Coco alongside them, aiming her Minolta with one hand, the loose horse just behind.

Sitting in meant that Jamie rode with the motion of the rising and falling back of the animal, his naked buttocks firmly glued to the saddle. Post trotting meant roughly the reverse, Queenie's bottom moving steadily up and down in rhythm with the beast. As her behind bounced, her vagina slid on Jamie's penis in much the same motion as she had made on top of Bobo in the hammock, with the difference that, as Jamie had announced, the horse was doing the work, like some powerful, living, fuck-machine.

It is most extraordinarily erotic, this horse-back copulation. Queenie rides Jamie's hot, solid, throbbing cock, with the wind and the sun on her back and naked buttocks, her fingers tight on his shoulders, her hair flying forwards, the sweaty smell of the horse mingling in her nostrils with the tanginess of the sea. As a background to the pleasing, regular, drumming of the hooves on hard-packed sand, Queenie is vaguely aware of the gentle swish of small waves breaking on the shore.

The effect of what is happening to her is to heighten her senses; she tries to be aware of everything. Occasionally she glances all around her; at Coco with her camera, two or three yards away; at the aquamarine, sparkling South China Sea; at the distant islands; at the white sands which slide beneath them, stretching endlessly behind the horses; at the riderless horse which happily trots after them; at the sumptuously green tiers of paddy-fields behind the dunes. But the majority of the time her eyes are cast downwards, riveted in horny fascination on her steady impaling, on Jamie's thick brown pubic thatch and his cock beneath it, on which she slides up and down, on the just-visible swollen sides of his jiggling balls.

When they have been going for more than three minutes, orgasm inexorably building within them both, Queenie slides one hand from Jamie's shoulder, reaching down between them, under his cock, to take hold of his balls, which she lovingly squeezes. 'I'll come if you do that!' he protests.

'So come!' she shouts deliriously, squeezing harder, and seconds later he does, warm semen gushing up inside her as she screams her own orgasm along with his, far louder than she has ever dared, or cared, to express an orgasm before, because it is ripping through her guts – and because there is no one out here to hear her, apart from themselves and the circling gulls.

As Jamie pulls the horse to a stop, laughter replaces orgiastic ecstasy. Happy, joyful, incredulous laughter, Queenie impaled on Jamie's wilting penis, astonished that such a thing could have occurred to her, at its amazing lasciviousness and almost unbearable beauty. They kiss and embrace, Queenie's eyes moist. Finally she climbs down, the first time she has got off both horse and cock simultaneously, and walks unsteadily to her own mount.

'We left our knickers at least a couple of kilometres back there,' Queenie, her face creased with laughter, pointed out as she heaved herself up into the saddle with a grunt.

'Bloody hell. Bloody, bloody hell!' exclaimed Coco, almost as affected by what she had been watching and photographing as they had been – raunchily turned on, but unsatisfied. 'It's all right for you two, but what the fuck about me?' she complained. 'Bloody hell!'

'Cool it. You're next,' said Jamie.

'Sure.' She nodded between his legs. 'Even you aren't going to get it up again that fast, Mister Australia. Cool it. Me and my gee-gee are going to have to!' Dismounting, she speedily stripped naked, covertly watching Jamie watching her as she did so. Getting back on the white stallion, she urged it into the sea, taking it out until it was swimming. Then, giggling, she managed the difficult – and dangerous – feat of standing up on the saddle and diving from it into the water.

'Shit!' grunted Jamie, alarmed. Cupping his hands over his mouth he bellowed, 'Stay well clear of those bloody hooves! They'll snap your leg clean through if they catch it.'

Coco survived her swim without mishap. As she emerged from the sea, a splendid vision of naked loveliness with her long black hair sticking to her breasts and shoulders in streaks, and tiny pearls of water trembling and shining amidst her pubic hairs, she said to Queenie and Jamie who, mounted, had watched her little adventure from beginning to end, 'You should get your shirts off. You look positively rude like that!'

'Okay now?' asked Jamie, as Coco's stallion followed her out, water streaming off its white coat.

'Better. The hots are cooled for the moment!'

'Great,' he said. 'Listen, I'm famished. I thought maybe we'd have lunch before your ride.'

'Yeah, let's do that.' Coco rolled her shorts, training shoes and socks into her shirt, tied the sleeves tight around them to make a bundle and, clutching it in one hand, swung herself nimbly into the saddle. 'But I didn't consent to my ride yet, remember?'

Jamie shrugged. 'So refuse!' he challenged.

Looking at him archly for a moment, she said nothing. Then she glanced down at herself and carefully arranged wet locks of hair so that they hid her nipples. 'Heh, get me,' she exclaimed. 'Lady Godiva!'

'Say no!'

'Race you back to your clothes,' Coco responded. With a whoop she urged her horse into a canter, then a full gallop, standing in the stirrups, leaning forward like a jockey.

Jamie caught only the occasional glimpse of the superbly erotic view of Coco's rear end, raised high criss-crossed with thin red stripes and fading little bruises from Helga's beating, black bush heavy beneath it, because damp sand was flying in thick, high arches from the stallion's hooves, and he was forced to turn his head to one side to keep it out of his eyes. He was unable to catch her, though Queenie almost did, aggravating his problem with the sand; his shirt front and face were daubed with it by the time they reached their scattered clothes. Panting, a radiant grin of exhilaration creasing his face, Jamie brushed himself off and climbed out of the saddle and into his pants and jeans. Leaving his boots on the beach he got barefoot on the horse as Queenie slipped from hers. 'We'll picnic right here,' he said. 'I'll fetch the hamper.'

When, fifteen minutes later, he returned, the wicker hamper balanced precariously in front of him behind the mare's neck, Queenie was also naked. Both girls were lying on their fronts, lower legs in the sea, chins on the backs of their hands, watching him. He clambered awkwardly from the horse and heaved the hamper to the sand. 'Jesus Christ,' he murmured, as he stared at the girls. 'It makes a guy real horny, two female arses striped like that!'

'You should have been there,' said Queenie.

'Nobody bloody invited me, did they?'

'Hey, you dirty bastard – stop looking at my bum!' exclaimed Coco. She rolled on to her back.

'Shit! At least put your knickers on for lunch?' he pleaded. 'A feller can stand only so much.'

'All right,' agreed Queenie. I'll put my shirt on as well. I rather enjoy being white.'

'Right on, spoilsport,' said Coco, getting up and going to her bundle of clothes.

Jamie spread a mini-feast on a cloth on the sand near the water's edge, where they tucked in to *lapu lapu inihaw*, which was cold grilled fish seasoned with salt, pepper, garlic and soya sauce, and *lumpia Shanghai* – small spring-rolls in soy sauce – washing it down with two bottles of Tapey, a rice wine which Jamie had had packed in ice. While they lunched he entertained them with stories about himself, of a life which, at only thirty-two, had already been packed with adventure. As a youth he had shown considerable academic prowess, yet he had opted out of Melbourne University, 'bored shitless' as he put it. He had started his working life ignominiously as a carbon-paper salesman, surprising the company, but not himself, by quickly becoming their biggest-selling salesman ever, using 'every fucking trick in the book'.

'Life's a jungle,' he told them. 'You have to go out there punching and weaving, ducking and diving, and make sure you stay ahead of the game.'

'Talking of games,' said Coco. 'We didn't tell you about Masters yet. He's playing one, and no mistake.'

Jamie groaned. 'Now what?'

'Oh, just a couple of things. Firstly, I was obliged to do him damage the other afternoon.'

Jamie's jaw dropped. 'You did him damage? Christ, girl, he's three times your bloody size!'

Queenie carefully sliced the end off a spring-roll as she said, 'Coco's an aikido expert.'

'I don't care if she's got a black belt in karate – the man's a fucking gorilla!'

119

'I was in their cabin with Luk,' Coco explained. 'She got seasick. I decided to have a quick peek through his things. He caught me.' She shrugged. 'He went for me so I threw him.'

'You threw him,' said Jamie flatly, in black-faced amazement.

'Yeah. I chopped the bastard in the neck first, and threw him.' She grinned. 'He went down real heavy!'

Jamie shook his head. 'Jesus – you're not just asking for trouble, doll, you're begging for it!'

'I haven't told you what I turned up. Two passports in different names – and a gun.'

'This doesn't exactly amaze and astound me. You might have guessed something like that without going and sticking your stupid little nose right into it.'

'Well, I did, and that's that.' Coco, on her knees, sipped her wine. 'Then one of your barmen was arrested yesterday afternoon. He was trying to smuggle some dope.'

'Yeah, Fidel Ramos. Poor sod. It happens from time to time; the temptation to make a quick killing's too much for them. Good barman, too. Good, as dead barman, now.' He paused. 'So?'

'We believe Masters and Li were behind it.'

'You do? Why?'

Queenie described the scene they had witnessed at the dockside. When she finished, he was looking savagely grim. 'Shit. It sure sounds like they were using Fidel as a courier. Son of a bitch! If that's true, there'll be others.' He paused, squinting into the sun, angry. 'If they're using my fucking boat to smuggle dope, and my crewmen to carry it on and off, I'll have the bastards castrated!'

'We tried to get hold of Helga for some straight talking,' said Coco, 'but she'd left the ship already. And she wasn't at breakfast this morning, or in her cabin. She's mixed up in this in some way almost certainly – but partner she's not.'

'Maybe she'll be back by this evening. We can talk then,' said Queenie.

'Damn it!' exclaimed Jamie. 'If she isn't, I might be tempted to have a little poke about in her cabin, and see

120

what I can turn up about the Helga connection.' He frowned at them both in turn. 'I warned you about staying well clear of possible bother – now you've even got me involved!'

'It looks like your ship's involved, Jamie,' Queenie pointed out. 'That being the case, it's just as well that we are possessed of these inquisitive brains of ours.'

He sighed. 'Sorry. You're right. And I'm going to have to do something about it, aren't I?'

'You bet.'

'I'm pissed off to hell about this, I tell you.' He swallowed down half a plastic cup of wine, and refilled it. 'Let's try and forget about it until we get back to the *Star*, shall we? Try and recapture our earlier mood.'

As they rounded off their meal with lanzones, which resembled small potatoes and had delicious, glassy fruit-flesh, Jamie explained to them how, three years previously, with only a stake of twenty thousand Australian dollars to his name, he had managed to persuade Bangkok bankers, tricky operators themselves, to put up the entire capital for his gambling-boat enterprise, with the help of certain financial assurances from his associate, and now firm friend, Dominic, Lord Bream.

'One more payment, that's all, and I own the *Star of Kowloon* and everything on her,' he said. He finished his fruit and wiped his lips on a serviette. 'That is, two-thirds of her's mine. One-third belongs to Nick.'

'That would make you a pretty wealthy guy, I guess?' said Coco.

'The business and the boat must be worth a handful of millions.' He shrugged. 'I'm not much of a boaster, but when I look around at the rat-race of this world, I get mighty proud of myself.'

'Hardly surprising,' commented Queenie. 'By the way, where is Dominic? I don't remember seeing him lately.'

'He stopped behind at Taipei. He had some business there. He happens to be brilliant with the Chinks.'

'Amongst other things,' said Queenie, the innuendo clear, as she thought about her evening with the two of them.

'Jesus, don't remind me. That was kinda weird, that night.'

'I told you, didn't I?' said Queenie to Coco.

He glared at her over his cup as he swigged down the last of the wine, then he screwed up the cup and threw it into the sea. 'What did you tell her?'

'No, nothing. It doesn't matter.'

But Jamie's composure was somewhat ruffled. 'Just what the hell did you tell her, Queenie?'

'Don't get your knickers in a twist. We always discuss our sexual adventures with one another, you know that. When I described to her that last bit – you know, the two of you in me – she said it must have been great. And I said I didn't think you'd let it happen again.'

'Oh, is that all?' He raised his face to the sun and closed his eyes. 'Yeah, well, I won't will I?'

'You enjoyed it. You said as much immediately afterwards.'

'Yeah, but . . .'

'There's nothing gay about it, Jamie,' Queenie insisted.

'Will you please shut up about it?'

'I see what you mean,' Coco said slowly to Queenie, deliberately teasing Jamie by the insinuating expression in her voice. 'He is sensitive about it, isn't he?'

'And you can just shut your pretty trap,' he said, opening his eyes. But he was grinning. He stood, unzipping his jeans. 'And get your knickers off right now, kid. I'll show you who's a fucking poof!' Within seconds he was naked, staring down at them, his penis flaccid. Coco was still calmly eating a lanzone, its juice trickling down from the corner of her lips. 'I said,' he insisted, 'get your gear off. We're going for a ride!'

'Then you'd better do something about that,' Coco responded saucily, pointing up at his penis with the remains of the lanzone.

'No, let me,' muttered Queenie, seized with a sudden urge at the sight of him. She slid her knickers down her legs, stepped out of them and closed in on Jamie on tiptoe, legs slightly apart, pushing her pubic mound into his penis, grinding her hips, kissing him, her tongue slipping inside his mouth, her hands clutching his buttocks. Moving her mouth off his, making it sound as deliberately dirty as she could, she muttered, 'Go on, filthy bastard. Give her a really good fucking, just like you belted me. Get on that horse and ram this' – her hand slid between them and she took firm hold of his rapidly rising penis – 'right up her sweet little cunt!'

She jerked on his cock as if she was shaking a dice-cup, and was gratified to feel it almost leap to attention. 'Good boy!' she said, a wicked smile cracking her dimple.

'Ready!' Coco called out gaily, as if she had just dressed for an evening out, rather than rid herself of her knickers.

'So are they,' said Queenie.

'They?'

'Jamie and Arnold!' She pulled Jamie, by his erection, towards his horse. 'On your bike, big boy!'

'Once you let go my banana.'

As soon as Jamie was back in the saddle, with Coco swinging up to face him, levity vanished. Coco, measurably keener for this experience than she had let on, performed the operation of impaling herself in one deft movement. Her leg went up and over the mare's neck, her foot bumping it on the way and, even as her toes slipped into the stirrup, one hand gripping Jamie's bicep, with the other she fisted his cock inside her. She sank down on it with a gasp of contentment, then sagged forward, both arms around him, her lips on his neck, and began bouncing her bottom.

Taking up the reins without a word, Jamie thumped the horse's ribs with his bare heels. It trotted briefly, then decided by itself to stretch into a canter, and he let it go.

Queenie was not even mounted. There was no chance of catching up even if she were, so she sank down into the sand, legs flat, leaning back on her hands, and watched with an amused, lecherous grin as horse and 'riding' riders raced off into the distance, clouds of sand arching high behind them.

Coco's coupling is markedly different from Queenie's.

At a fast canter the animal is a most comfortable ride; its legs stretching to their full extent, its paces are enormous and its back remains almost as smooth as if it were flying. Coco's hair is streaming out over one of Jamie's shoulders, he leans well forward, into her, and she leans backwards, her hands linked together behind his broad back; in this attitude she finds she can be almost still on his cock, or she can ride it with long, slow, easy motions. She does both, a smile of the purest ecstasy – which he cannot see because her cheek is buried in his shoulder – on her face. She discovers, as had Queenie, that this naked copulation astride the back of a fine animal, as they speed through sublime scenery, is one of the headiest things that has ever happened to her.

Jamie grits his teeth into the warm breeze, nostrils flaring, adrenalin seething, as it does even in normal circumstances with the exhilaration of a gallop, savouring the incredible combination of riding a thoroughbred horse whilst a mixed-race but superb example of young womanhood rides him.

They fuck and gallop in this fashion for more than five minutes, then the animal begins to loose speed. It is tired; it's been working hard, and there are two of them. Recognising that the mare is in need of rest, Jamie pulls her up. 'Must we stop?' moans Coco, sinking down on him as far as she can, her orgasm an approaching shadow.

'Don't want to kill the beast,' he replies. Taking Coco by the buttocks he lifts her easily off him, raising her high so that her bush is level with his mouth. He plants a kiss amongst her pubic hairs, then twists sideways and lets her slide down his body and the side of the panting horse, to the sand. He dismounts.

The animal's flanks ooze foamy white perspiration; there is more sweat thick around its bridle straps. It wanders slowly off towards the paddy-fields in search of water, as Jamie takes Coco by the hand, leads her down the slope of the beach, lies her on her back where sea and sand meet, opens her hot thighs wide, lets himself down with his elbows sinking in wet sand on either side of her shoulders, and, as water sweeps past them to the depth of his forearms, lowers his crotch to hers.

'Put it in,' he murmurs. Coco reaches between her legs, finds his penis and fists it inside her vagina. She is intensely keyed up from the copulating ride; they both are; they pant almost as hard as the horse. His bottom bucks and heaves as the sea-level rises and falls around them, at its deepest submerging their genitals, cooling them, seeping inside her – another sweet kick. Their climax is most powerful; they both shout, causing a flock of gulls which had settled on the beach not far away to rise into the air in pandemonium.

Laughing, giving themselves no time for recovery, Jamie rolls them over and over together into the water until, floating, they drift apart and begin to lazily, contentedly swim.

More than an hour had elapsed before – Coco mounted behind Jamie on the flanks of the horse, the animal walking slowly – they returned to Queenie. Except for her feet, she was covered up against the sun, sitting with bare toes at the water's edge.

'Where've you two been – Australia?' Queenie asked.

'Further – to the moon and back,' Coco told her dreamily.

'Aint that the fucking truth!' said Jamie.

# 8

# No Buzz Like a Show Buzz

'Oh, shit,' exclaimed Coco as she stepped inside their suite early that evening, 'we've been turned over, God damn it!'

The cabin was in a distressing mess: all the drawers and cupboards rifled and their contents strewn all over the place, the stateroom turned upside-down, clothes scattered over the carpet and the bed.

'Please not the jewellery,' said Queenie, invaded with a sinking feeling. Both of them had some lovely pieces; there was some valuable antique family gold in her own box.

Though their jewellery had been rummaged through, it seemed to be intact. What were missing, though – and that seemed the full extent of the robbery, for even Coco's valuable photographic equipment was still there – were most of the prints and all of the negatives of the pictures Coco had so far shot on the trip.

'That's just terrific!' she exclaimed at this discovery. 'I'll have to begin all over again.' She looked angrily round the stateroom. 'Masters, of course, bastard. Who else?'

'I suppose so,' said Queenie. 'When you let us in, did the door seem tampered with?'

'I don't think so. Let's take a look.'

There was no indication that the door had been forced in any way.

Queenie stated the obvious. 'Somebody used a key.'

'Let's get Jamie.'

Surveying the wrecked suite ten minutes later, Jamie said, 'Yeah, I'd say it was Masters for sure. He was looking for evidence that you might be more than you claim. He took the photographs for good measure.'

'Then, Jesus, he's got that evidence, even though we're not more than we claim,' Coco pointed out.

'How's that?'

'A whole pile of it. Shots of him and Li going into and coming out of that opium den . . . the spare picture I kept of him at the craps table . . . the dockside scene. I don't see him believing the truth – that it was merely coincidence plus amateur curiosity.'

Jamie grunted. He walked back into the cabin, hands stuffed in his jeans pockets, frowning at the chaos. 'You're in it right up to your necks, aren't you, my pets?' he threw over his shoulder.

'Kinda,' agreed Coco, following him.

'Would you know your way around a gun?'

'What's this now – theatricals?' said Queenie.

He turned around. 'Hardly. These creeps are for real. They're dangerous, kid. If they've decided you're a branch of the law on their backs, they're not going to come begging on bended knees for you to please go away. They're gonna blow you away.'

'Mmmm.' Queenie stared hard at him as realisation dawned. 'You're right.' She produced a twisted smile. 'One of the three religions of the gentry is shooting,' she said. 'Huntin', shootin' and fishin' says it all.' She paused. 'I'm actually very good with a gun.'

'And I've shot plastic ducks in fairgrounds,' said Coco.

Jamie laughed. 'I'll get you a handgun anyway. One each. They may not do more than try to warn you off. On the other hand don't open the cabin door to anyone without being on your guard. I'll fetch the guns now. I've got a small armoury locked away in case of any attempted pirate raid. On my way I'll have a quick shufti through

Helga's cabin, if she isn't back aboard yet. See you here in about half an hour.'

Later, whilst showing Coco how to use the Browning automatic he brought her, Jamie commented, 'Hell, has she got some horny gear, that Helga creature. Jesus Christ, there's stuff in her wardrobe to turn a guy on without a chick being inside it!'

Queenie smiled. 'And? What did you find out?'

'That she's a raving lessie into S and M!'

'Oh, brilliant of you!'

'I discovered not a thing. She'll have her passport with her, of course. She couldn't get off the boat without it. There was nothing to tell me anything about her except her gear.'

'We've absolutely got to have a talk with her as soon as she comes aboard,' said Queenie. 'You do realise that Masters' got Coco's photos of her waiting near the opium den – and going in? Depending on her role, that could spell danger for her.'

'Too right. You and your bloody camera, Coco.'

Coco shrugged. 'What is done, is done. How do you suppose Masters got in here? The door wasn't forced.'

'If he's got contacts amongst the crew – guys working for him – it wouldn't have been too difficult to get hold of a pass key. I've just used one, and there are several others.' He paused. 'Keep your door very firmly locked on the inside at all times.'

'I hope we're exaggerating the danger,' said Queenie.

'So do I, but I doubt it.' Jamie glanced at his watch. 'It's seven. Fancy Manila tonight?'

'Sure. I don't think we want to stay aboard again.'

'I'll take you. But leave your handbag behind. I'll tuck your cash into my money belt. And don't bother with a camera, Coco. It'll be a target. The place is a nest of thieves.'

They took a jeepney into the Ermita district, the most popular area of Manila for tourists, and in places as colourful as the jeepney itself. Traffic was chaotic. Their driver hooted and honked his way through an incredible assortment of public transport vehicles, all of them gaudily painted: trishaws – bicycles with sidecars; tricycles – similar to trishaws but with covered motorcycles or mopeds providing the power; taxis with and without meters; battalions of jeepneys; and calesas – two-wheeled horse-cabs.

The noise, close to unbearable, was totally dominated by car horns, and Jamie explained that this din was particularly aggravated by the fact that countless taxi meters were rigged in such a way that every time the drivers honked their horns a unit was added to the meter, which was electronically linked to facilitate this blatant trickery.

They dined at a table on the pavement outside the Food Fiesta Restaurant, on the busy corner of Malvar and J. Bocobo streets, engrossed in watching the lively crowds and commenting on various characters. For after-dinner entertainment Jamie offered them the choice of pubs, a faith-healing demonstration, a body-to-body massage parlour, or a live sex show.

'You're really trying to complicate our lives, aren't you?' remarked Queenie. 'Booze, religion or sex!'

'All three, if you like,' said Jamie. 'Tell you what, they have these darling little sheilas in the massage parlours, real honeys. You get naked and they get naked and . . .'

'Cut it out, Jamie,' Coco interrupted. 'You're sex mad! Let's go to a pub and decide what to do from there.'

'You gone off sex?'

'I should have thought you'd had quite enough for one day!'

'What me? Nah, never can get enough!' He grinned boyishly and stood up, cupping his hand under an elbow of each of them, and drawing them to their feet.

'Come on, I'll take you to the Kangaroo Club.'

'Trust an Aussie,' said Queenie.

They had a couple of rounds of drinks in the noisy, crowded, smoky pub, whose clientele on that evening was largely composed of American servicemen having a night out from the base at Angeles. When a group of them tried, not surprisingly, to muscle in on the girls, Jamie good-naturedly hustled Queenie and Coco out of there.

'Looks like the massage parlours are going to be doing great business later,' he said, in the street.

'Seems a good enough reason to stay away from them,' commented Queenie. 'So where shall we go?'

'Didn't you mention something about faith healing?' asked Coco.

'I did. I did.'

'I vote that we forget that, then, and visit a sex show!' she said brightly, making them laugh.

From the outside there was nothing to suggest that the place he took them to, in a back alley, offered any sort of show at all. Saying, 'This is the real McCoy. Cory Aquino's been clamping down, so they're dead cautious,' he pressed a bell by the side of the tired-looking wooden door. A spyhole opened, an eye surveyed them for several seconds, a bolt scraped, the door creaked open, and was relocked behind them as soon as they entered the ill-lit little foyer.

'Not exactly the Crazy Horse, is it?' said Queenie, wrinkling her nose in distaste as Jamie passed some money over to the man who had let them in. His one eye which had examined them through the peephole was, oddly enough, his only one; the other was covered by a black patch.

'Sleazeville. But a heavily raunchy show last time I was here,' Jamie retorted. 'Made the Crazy Horse look like a chimpanzees' tea-party.'

After descending a flight of worn-carpeted stairs, they found themselves in a large basement with a scattering of small round tables and chairs, several of which were occupied. The lights were predominantly red. They were led to a table adjacent to a small uncurtained stage – with nothing to adorn it but a large bed, some cushions and a couple of rugs – while the taped voice of Billie Holiday sang the slow, sentimental ballad 'But Beautiful', filling the smoky air with melodious sounds from almost forty years before.

Queenie had experienced a certain amount of trepidation on first entering such a dive, but when she saw that there were several other females around, though few of them

130

young, she became as relaxed as Coco – who had quickly taken her seat, bubbling with eagerness. The tablecloth, Queenie noticed, was freshly laundered; there was, surprisingly, a little bowl of flowers on it. They ordered champagne, which arrived in a shining ice-bucket on a stand, and the glasses were clean and expensive.

In another half an hour the place was fairly full. There seemed to be a hushed expectancy in the air; conversation was more sporadic and more subdued than it would have been amongst an audience awaiting a floor-show in an ordinary nightclub. An odd sort of an atmosphere, Queenie decided, as if most of the customers felt a bit guilty about being there.

The music stopped and the beginning of the show was heralded by a few seconds' complete blackout and silence. Then a single, discus-sized white spot cut across the club to fall on a bare, white female behind. As it rested there, two hands with long mauve nails stole into the light from either side of the spot, clutching beneath the buttocks. The spot grew in size to illuminate fleshy thigh tops and crimson suspenders and a heavy brown bush nestling between the thighs, as the fingertips stretched apart the labia and opened the vagina.

The spot quickly expanded to drape light over a girl who knelt on the bed, her cheek flat on it, her back to the audience, panties at half-mast on chubby thighs, and a skirt piled up on her hips. Queenie gasped, as did several others. She had anticipated some sort of routine striptease to begin with, not this shockingly immediate, blatant sexual exposure.

As the girl stretched her vagina further apart, wiggling her bottom while she did so, a black hand appeared out of the darkness, in it a white, whirring vibrator, which it inserted deep in the girl's pussy, before vanishing.

Music began, Joe Cocker's 'Unchain My Heart'. The girl took hold of the vibrator, pulled it out of herself, ran its tip around her pussy lips, before poking it into her bottom hole as two fingers of her other hand slipped deep into her vagina. For perhaps a minute she played with herself in

131

this way, fingers sliding in and out in the opposite direction to the bottom-breaching vibrator, a sensual see-saw motion in time to the music. Then she stopped, unplugged herself, sat back on her haunches, and turned around on her knees to face the audience, presenting them with an unexpectedly lovely, artless smile and drawing hesitant applause.

It was a good beginning, one which achieved its purpose of shocking the audience into sitting up and taking notice. More spots came on, red and blue and green, colours overlapping colours, a surprisingly skilful use of lighting. Standing, the girl – small, just a little plump, a Filipino – unclipped her skirt. Jerking her hips rhythmically to the final bars of 'Unchain My Heart', she let the skirt fall, then, facing the audience, she opened her thighs wide and inserted the vibrator up inside herself once more – all the way in until only an inch or so protruded. Falling back on the bed, she propped herself on the cushions and began masturbating with the device. Presumably, she was acting out her ecstasy but, with her long-lashed eyelids closed, her tongue rolling around over full lips, and a hand twisting and turning at nipples which protruded above a scarlet quarter-cup bra, she put on a convincing performance of approaching orgasm.

Finally, she shuddered from head to foot, her toes clenching, and she moaned loudly. Her hands stilled, her eyes opened, and a contented, wicked grin split her face as the lights went out and the club was plunged in total blackness, filled with rather more enthusiastic applause than before.

Moments later, more Joe Cocker: a slow, throbbing, sensuous beat, the bass pounding, good, sexy, bluesy stuff. Then pale blue and white spots go up and mix together on the bed, where two girls in scanty underwear are locked in one another's arms, kissing. A long, steamy, lesbian scene unfolds. As they get themselves naked, and then head-to-tail, in an apparently eager *soixante-neuf*, their actions produce the effect which the first girl, despite her raunchy attempts at sincerity, failed to do, of arousing Jamie, Queenie and Coco.

The session is a lengthy one, almost half an hour. They simulate orgasm, or perhaps they really do climax; the place is plunged into darkness once more and, when the applause dies down, Jamie mutters, 'Hot stuff, no? They offer the best here. There'll be just one more act, the hottest, planned to leave you panting for more.'

'Yikes. That was real horny,' remarks Coco. Her thighs are jammed together over a hand whose fingers dig into her dress at the crotch and, unseen beneath the table, softly probe.

'The finale's guaranteed to be a sizzler,' said Jamie. 'There'll be at least one stud.'

As it turned out, there were three. A trio of tall, muscular negroes and black soul music to match – Percy Sledge, 'When A Man Loves A Woman'. Looking like a song-and-dance act, the men, each of them in tight white jeans with white shirts knotted around their muscle-rippling bellies, sway in time to the music. A voluptuous young woman, with platinum-blonde hair cascading over her shoulders, appears, a blue spot tracking her progress across the stage, and the music changes to Tina Turner, 'Crazy About You Baby'. The girl – who could be American; she is certainly not oriental – writhes and undulates sexily amongst the hip-rocking negroes, snaking her black-miniskirt-encased haunches, fingering the men's biceps, their bellies, their thighs in loving admiration.

The four of them continue this erotic dance throughout the number, then, as Brook Benton begins to croon 'Rainy Night In Georgia', the blonde sinks to her knees at the side of the man on the left of the group, turns him by his thighs so that the back of her head will not block the audience's view, and slowly slides down his zipper. Her blue eyes sweep over the club as she does this. She licks her lips with a half-smile as if to say – You see what I'm up to? – drags his jeans down his thighs, follows them with dazzling white slips, and engulfs his penis in her mouth.

When, half a minute later, the man is fully erect, she walks on her knees to the next, who is already on his way up by the time his pants are down. As she completes the job with lips and fingers, Brook Benton fading into Ike and Tina Turner's 'So Fine', the first stud strips naked while she travels on her knees to the third who, wearing no underpants, springs to impressive attention as soon as his jeans are open. Nevertheless she treats him to a quick rub and suck for good measure.

Queenie's eyes are popping, she can hardly believe what she is witnessing. Almost without realising it, she has undone the top of her Givenchy slacks. By the time all three negroes are naked, still hip-swaying to the music, their cocks, much the same commendable size, swaying straight out in front of them, Queenie's hand is very firmly into the waistband of her slacks and her fingers are going to work.

Even more turned on by this lubricious display than Queenie, Coco whimpers a little orgasm, managing to bring herself to this state despite the fact that her hand has got into no more intimate contact with her pussy than through the material of both dress and knickers.

Jamie, vaguely aware what the girls are up to, realises that the reflected light from the spots gives just enough illumination to make out, with concentration, what the shadowy shapes around him might be doing. He keeps one hand very firmly on the table and the other wrapped around his champagne glass. But his erection swells to stretch his trousers as he watches the blonde, who, on her knees in front of one man, who has sat down on the edge of the bed, takes his cock in her mouth, whilst the other two, kneeling on either side of her, hoist her skirt up, and tug down her knickers. With her drooping panties clinging to her thighs below stocking-tops and suspenders, she sucks avidly on, while four hands, very black indeed against her soft white flesh, plunder her buttocks and inner thighs.

They are fine specimens of manhood, all three of these studs, nowhere near as big as him, but they remind Queenie of her steamy session with the chief engineer. As one of the men gets on his knees behind the girl and impales her, her fellatio unabated, three of Queenie's fingers are plunging deep inside her pussy.

The show continues in a heavy, breathless atmosphere, backed by non-stop soul music – black bodies glistening sweat, moving in hypnotically slow motion. The blonde is stripped naked; she slips back on to her high-heeled shoes after having suspenders and stockings removed.

The routine hots up. When all three men have fucked her, the girl prepares for a classic three-way penetration, straddling one man on the bed, guiding his cock in her, while another squats in front of her face, erection hovering. Jamie suddenly becomes acutely aware of Coco's fingers working on his flies beneath the table. His massive hard-on is too desperate to be free for him to try and stop her, nevertheless he glances around with a touch of nervous embarrassment as her hand dives beneath his pants. Of course, every eye in the audience is rooted on the spectacle. Many hands have found genitals by now. This is no tired, third-rate performance going on up there, it is red-hot stuff.

Jamie's cock is snugly encased in Coco's fist by the time the third stud drops to his knees behind the girl, who is now servicing the other two with mouth and pussy. He lubricates his penis with Johnson's Baby Oil, a plastic bottle of which he has produced from beneath the mattress, closes and drops the bottle, and carefully begins to cram his cock in beside his companion's.

This is clearly going to be the finale; his own finale is on its way for Jamie, too. Queenie is sagging in her seat, her fingers have slipped out of herself, and she watches the end approach with semi-glazed eyes as Coco builds herself up for her second orgasm while she brings Jamie to his first.

The rhythm of the music changes. Appropriately George McCrae sings the ultrasexy 'Rock You Baby', and the three negroes climax in turn, obeying the edict of the porn business all over the world – never waste a come-shot – one unplugging the girl and shooting over her buttocks and back; the second over her face and in her mouth; the third, as the others fall away, pulling out of her, rolling her over on to her back, kneeling and erupting over her belly and breasts.

The lights dim, very slowly, as the blonde, smiling at an audience she cannot see, smears the semen across her flesh. Jamie's sperm splashes against the underside of the table. He grunts, and Coco – Coco squeaks. But they are by no means the only people in the room now making sexual noises; the club is alive with them.

It is dark. The music ends. There is a semi-stupefied rustling in the air, a few final grunts and moans, a muttering and murmuring, and not one single hand-clap. The management, aware of what has happened to the audience – what else is the performance for but carnal arousal? – switch the music from soul to Sade, and wait a considerable length of time before putting on the lights.

The stage, stripped of its show and its lighting effects, appears more tawdry than before, the bed a rumpled mess, the baby-oil bottle lying on the floor, propped against a cushion, one corner of the rug doubled over on itself. Queenie gazes at it misty-eyed, as if she is still seeing the performers at it – as, indeed, she is. Coco shoots a lecherous grin at Jamie as she wipes the side of her hand with a Kleenex while Jamie, who is always mightily aroused in this place, but has never gone to the extreme of masturbation whilst here, looks a little sheepish.

'Gee, was that ever the horniest . . . wow!' exclaims Coco. She puffs out her cheeks. 'What a day!'

'Beats faith healing,' mutters Queenie.

Jamie hauled the champagne bottle from a sea of slopping, melting ice, but when he upended it over his glass, only a tiny drop fell out. 'I am fucking parched,' he mumbled. He waved the bottle in the air, calling for a waiter, then managed a weak grin. 'Massage parlour next then?' he said.

'Go to hell!' said Coco.

# 9

# Bonk, Bonk. Bonk, Bonk. *Bonk!*

The following morning, Dominic, who had flown down from Taipei to rejoin the *Star of Kowloon*, took breakfast with Jamie and the girls. Jamie put him in the picture about Masters, Li and Helga. They were all anxious to tackle Helga, but she had not yet returned; nor had Masters and Li. But, then, the ship was not due to sail off on its way south until the late afternoon.

Helga did not board until after lunch, a bare twenty minutes after the Englishman and his Chinese sidekick. Coco happened to be buying a magazine at a shop near the ship's main boarding and muster-point, when Masters appeared. The look to which he treated her was so fierce and threatening that her spine prickled, but she managed to gather up enough courage to shrug and frown right back.

Having spotted Helga coming aboard from the bridge, Jamie intercepted her on her way to her cabin, and she agreed to meet him for what he described as a quiet tête-à-tête shortly afterwards in the bar – neglecting to mention that Dominic and Queenie and Coco would be there, too.

When it was almost time for the meeting, Queenie left Coco still fixing herself up. Simply dressed in a white cotton T-shirt and a cream below-the-knee pencil skirt with shell buttons all the way down the front, a low-budget outfit from Hilary Alexander in which she managed to look a million dollars, she made her way up.

Turning a corner at a junction of companionways, and about to go up a deck, Queenie bumped slap into Chief Engineer Bobo on his way down. He was dressed in spotless white shirt, jeans and trainers, instantly reminding her of the three studs in the sex show – and of their own earlier encounter in the hammock. The unexpected contact caused a tremendous thrill to run through her. Staring down at her with dark, brooding eyes from the bottom step of the next companionway, he uttered three simple words which were somehow charged with innuendo, and added to her thrill.

'Well, how nice,' he said flatly, as his eyes invaded her T-shirt.

His shirtsleeves were short, too tight for his bulging biceps. The shirt was unbuttoned almost to the waist: a thin gold chain with a tiny, glinting gold coin rested on his huge pectoral muscles. To her he seemed to exude a male smell of virile excitement.

'Hello,' she murmured, catching his eyes and holding them with her own, though swallowing hard.

'Going somewhere special?' he asked.

'Just for a drink.'

He said nothing more for long seconds, which might have been minutes, but their interlocked eyes communicated it all. Then, the inevitability of it almost blowing Queenie's mind, he said very firmly, clearly expecting no argument, 'I have an hour or so free before we sail. If you want a drink, there's plenty in my cabin, but I doubt we'll need it. Come.' The words went straight to her libido.

Slipping past her after one last, unmistakable look of burning lust, Bobo continued his journey down to the bowels of the boat, and Queenie, an aroused automaton – here was an unexpected, unheralded encounter impossible to resist! – followed a few steps behind him.

Never once did he look around, but he sensed her presence because, when he reached the door to his cabin, his broad back towards her still, he swung it open and stepped aside for her. As she passed him he gave her a most thorough goosing, scrunching up the linen-viscose of her skirt into the softness between her buttocks, fingers crawling all the way underneath her and probing there, causing her sensations which made her open her mouth, throw her head back, arch her back and sag at the knees. In this way he shoved her inside with his big hand, clanged the steel door shut behind them with his foot, then took her firmly by her shoulders, spun her around and lowered his fleshy, soft lips to hers.

As their mouths parted, his groin pressing into her pelvis, full hard-on digging at her belly, hand slipping back to her buttocks, he muttered, 'I've been going a little nuts thinking about the last time.' He pulled her even tighter on to him. 'I've even wanked on the memory. I don't often.'

'Undress me,' she gasped, frantic for closer contact, throat constricting, pussy already very damp. 'Please?' He dropped to his knees in front of her and, taking his time over it, from the bottom upwards undid the nine shell buttons, beginning at her knee. Her legs were bare. He trailed his tongue up the inside of a thigh as the material parted, teasing her by wiggling it from side to side as it got closer to its prize, while she gazed down at the black, tight-curled hair on the top of his head, and her insides began to melt away.

The last button. Simple, white, semi-transparent Miss Selfridge knickers prettily exposed, coppery pubic hairs curling around their edges. Eyes transfixed by this wholly arousing sight, he gasps, 'I thought it was red. But it was so dark the other day.' His fingers clawing into the waistband, he yanks the panties down, folding them over themselves on her thighs. Hands hooked over the fold, pubic bush inches from his nose, he grunts, 'The sweetest little red pussy!' then pulls her on to his mouth with her knickers, stretching them, tongue slipping under the thatch and finding her wetness as she produces one of the most long-drawn-out moans of her sexual life, and clamps her quivering thighs around his chin.

Queenie would be happy for him to stay down there

pussy-worshipping for ever, and for long, delicious moments he does just that, sliding his busy tongue deep up inside her as he gentles her clitoris with the ball of his thumb, licking and sucking her clitoris whilst finger-fucking her with one hand and plundering her buttocks with the other, thoroughly wetting her bush with his saliva, and breathing hot air through it. She mutters and moans indistinguishable words of sex, being driven almost insane with the lust of it.

Finally, his mouth leaves her. He unclips her suede belt, opens the fastener at the top of the skirt, drops the skirt to the floor where it piles around her feet, pushes her back on the bed – the hammock is not strung up – hastily unzips his jeans, lowers them, erection swaying, pushes Queenie's legs high and wide with his palms behind her knees, and falls upon her with a savage, gleeful grunt.

'Queenie not here yet?' said Coco, as she joined Jamie and Dominic at a table in the bar, carefully crossing her legs. 'That's a bit odd – she said she was coming up a quarter of an hour ago.'

Dominic's eyes flickered admiringly over her. 'I haven't seen her – and I've been here for ten minutes myself.'

'Very strange.' She raised an eyebrow at the barman with a 'service please?' smile. 'I guess she bumped into someone. So where's Helga?'

'Right there.' Jamie nodded in the direction of the door. Helga, in scarlet and black leather, her blonde hair, for once, swept high, perfectly coiffured, was making a most impressive entrance. She wore scarlet culottes of the finest kid, a matching loose top, and impossibly high-heeled black leather boots. She managed to walk, even on those heels, with regal authority, one hand on snaking hip, gold hoop earrings the size of saucers swaying. From somewhere she had suddenly acquired a Yorkshire terrier which she wore, rather than carried, under one arm.

'Good grief,' muttered Dominic, while she was still out of earshot. 'So that's the famous Helga!' He whistled quietly to himself.

As the men got to their feet, she reached them, at the same time as the barman, with the words, 'No, please be sitting. Perhaps someone is ordering me a daiquiri with double the rum?'

Stooping, she offered her cheek to Coco for a kiss, as Jamie ordered the drinks.

'My darlink,' she purred, 'I discover you as divine as always. So long without to see you, it is a human tragedy!' Kiss received, she curled herself into a chair, the tiny dog settling docilely in her lap. 'So, what is this urgency, Captain Bond?'

'Mister Bond, but call me Jamie,' said the ship's master. 'Meet Dominic, my associate.'

Formalities over, Coco took Helga's hand in both of hers, leaning forward.

'A lot of funny things have been going on on this boat, Helga,' she confided. 'We have to have a very, very serious, straight talk.'

Helga frowned, blinking her long lashes rapidly. 'Serious? What is this serious? What has Helga to do with serious?'

'That's what we mean to find out,' said Jamie. 'Let me spell it out to her, huh, Coco?'

'Okay. Shoot.'

'Our suspicions kinda started in a side alley back in Taipei . . .' began Jamie, as the barman appeared with a loaded tray. He told her all they knew, Helga not interrupting once, but her expression becoming graver and graver, her green eyes, with their greener shadow, occasionally flitting nervously around the bar as she listened.

'. . . so, that's just about it,' Jamie finished. 'The *Star of Kowloon* is a highly successful business, our business. The last thing we need is trouble, and having my crewmen involved with a drug-running operation is looking for some of the biggest trouble around. I want those guys Masters and Li off this boat, but I don't have proof. They've paid their passage, so I can't just chuck them off. It scares the shit out of me to even consider bringing in the Filipino police.' He paused, staring at the German girl. 'You know a great deal, Helga, I'm convinced. And, from what I gather from Queenie and Coco, you're sure as hell not involved with the creeps.' He took a sip of his lager, studying her some more. 'So, what gives?'

She returned his stare pensively for long seconds, one hand absently twisting the daiquiri glass on the table by its stem, the other stroking her dog. Then she said, 'Shit!'

'Yeah, shit,' echoed Coco. 'And we're in it.'

'I have to tell you that these men are as dangerous as you believe, no?' Picking up the glass she sipped the daiquiri through a straw, her eyes roving again as she appeared to be trying to make up her mind. 'Very well,' she said at last. 'What I am saying must be kept most confidential, you understand?'

'Of course. My business could be at stake,' said Jamie.

'Ja. Well, I am attached to the Hong Kong police force. We are working very closely with Interpol.'

There was a little gasp from Coco, but Jamie merely nodded. 'I kind of had something like that figured. It almost had to be.'

'Masters and Li are far bigger fish than you have been imagining. What you have unwittingly stumbled across is but a small part of their operation. Significant, but small. Using some of your crew members to carry for them. This finances them and their gambling, but in the meantime they have been busy setting up one of the biggest networks in the Far East.' Coco was staring at her, open-mouthed. 'Why do you gawp, darling? I am an undercover policewoman, this is all. We are all over the world.' She smiled, patting Coco's bare knee. 'Anyway, your face like that, it makes you prettier than ever!'

'It's not just the policewoman thing,' Coco told her. 'It's your accent. All of a sudden it almost vanished?'

'It is hardly necessary now amongst ourselves, is it? Horrible exaggeration, but for sure no one would believe that such a woman, with such an accent could be what I am.' She leant close to Coco and whispered in her ear, just loud enough for the others to hear. 'But don't worry, my dear. The sex, you can be sure, was no act!'

Coco grinned. 'Really? Could have fooled me!'

'Yes, Helga?' said Jamie, after a gentle cough. 'So, what's next? I repeat, they now have photos of you hanging around an opium den in Taipei – and going inside – amongst other pictures of themselves at the same place.'

Helga clucked her tongue. 'This, of course, is most annoying.'

'God, had I known. I'm sorry, Helga,' said Coco.

Coco's knee received another patting. 'Well, you did not. It's done and you must not blame yourself. With luck they will be thinking that perhaps it was coincidence. Helga the crazy lessie after something to smoke, no? They will check me out, this is for sure. They will find nothing.'

'But what do we do, Helga?' insisted Jamie.

'Okay. Let me explain the position concisely. My brief is to pinpoint their main distributors, warehouses, factories, et cetera. We have, and it has taken almost a year, pinned their Hong Kong bases down. I seem to have sorted out Taiwan, and I've just had reasonable success in Manila. But we are not quite ready to move in on them yet. We want to clean up the entire operation in one sweep, and that means just one more important location – where you are headed next, Legaspi City in South Luzon. This is a hopping-off place by boat for all the South Philippine Islands, and there is a lot of cocaine moving through there. Once I have got that sorted out, then the Hong Kong police department and Interpol will seize everybody at once.'

Jamie considered. He was looking far from happy. 'So,' he said. 'I let them stay aboard, knowing what I now know, with the accompanying danger to Queenie and Coco. We stop off as scheduled at Marinduque Island and then at Magnog, before rounding the coast to Legaspi, and each time we do some poor arsehole crewman runs the risk of life imprisonment or even death for running dope ashore for them while I do nothing?'

'I know how you feel. But at least you can be sure that there is no danger to your enterprise. We know you are clean. I ask only for two or three more days. Then, hopefully, we swoop.'

Jamie sighed. 'I guess I could have every man searched as he disembarks, then again as he boards.'

'And thus alert Masters and Li that someone is most probably on their tail? They will go quiet like mice, and I will have no chance of finding the Legaspi City connection.'

'You're using my boat as if it's a branch of the flaming Hong Kong police!' Jamie swore beneath his breath. 'And what if some other poor bastard Filipino crewman gets busted in the meanwhile?'

She produced a sad smile. 'Tough titty, ain't it, as I believe you Aussies are fond of saying. They know the risks, Jamie.' She paused. 'Cocaine is a seriously debilitating drug. Abused at its worst it destroys the brain. It kills. I am dedicated to do what I can to help stop its trade.'

Coco was goggling at her, which she clearly noticed. 'Sorry, Helga,' Coco said, 'but I find it hard to believe that there's this side to you.'

'Oh, *ja*, this is for real.' But Helga's hand returned to Coco's knee and slid a little under her skirt. She smiled disarmingly. 'It is half of me. The other half of me is also real – the sex maniac, no?'

Dominic looked positively startled, and even seriously concerned Jamie raised a grin.

Coco said, 'Yeah, well, talking of sex maniacs, where the hell is Queenie?'

Down in Bobo's hole of a cabin, Queenie is naked. The chief engineer is, too, with the exception of his short, white shirt which is unbuttoned all the way down. Having brought themselves to speedy orgasms with unbridled rutting, the two of them have briefly rested. Lust fires, quenched only temporarily, have blazed anew and they are at it again.

Queenie kneels on the bed as Bobo stands by it, watching greedily while Queenie brings him to erection with her mouth, copper head swaying, shining tresses bouncing over her shoulders, one hand cupping his balls, two fingers and the thumb of the other hand teasing the root of his penis.

144

There is no quicker way for him to raise a hard-on, this Zulu Indian, than to have a beautiful bare-arsed white chick with rose-painted lips sucking on his cock as he watches and savours, drinking in every second of it. In no time at all it is up and solid as a rubber truncheon. Queenie, engrossed, sucks happily on.

A short while later, after draining his second Foster's lager, Jamie remarked, 'My natural inclination is to believe you, Helga. What you told us has the ring of truth about it. But my ma always said never to trust a stranger, and my ship's on the line here. Can we see some ID?'

'I don't think that's quite necessary, is it?' said Dominic, mildly. 'Being the Aussie gentleman again, is it?'

'No, no – he's right,' said Helga. 'The way things go in that murky drug world out there, I could even be working for the Triads, since Masters and Li have been moving in on some of their territory.'

'The Triads?' Jamie whistled. 'They're tangling with the Triads? That's practically suicidal.'

'*Ja*. Well, they have a tougher team than what you know.' She whisked the Yorkie off her lap and stood up. 'My credentials are in my cabin. I can get them or . . .' her eyes ran, in what seemed to be thoughtful interest, over the three of them. '. . . you could come and see them. Ja – why do not we all go and have another drink there?'

Inside Helga's cabin, as he stripped the ring from another Foster's, Jamie confessed, 'I let myself in here last night and went through your gear, Helga.' He shrugged. 'Sorry. You weren't aboard. It was kind of an emergency.'

'It is understood.' She arched an eyebrow. 'You found not one thing incriminating, is this not so?'

Jamie grinned. 'That depends what I want to accuse you of!'

With a deep-throated laugh, Helga dropped the dog, which walked straight to a small rug, curled up and settled down to sleep on it. 'But you already knew, of course, of my preferences, from your intimacies with Queenie and

Coco, is this not so?' She perched herself on the bed next to Coco, and put an arm around her shoulders, squeezing. 'Is this not so, my dear?'

'Um ... yup,' said Coco. Suddenly, in the intimacy of this familiar cabin, with these people, she was beginning to feel slightly horny. She had experienced some incredible lesbian sex here with Helga and Queenie, she had been thoroughly screwed by Jamie, and even Dominic was not an unknown factor since Queenie had described her session with him and Jamie in most intimate detail. Helga, she remembered, had confessed that her lascivious activities were not reserved simply for women. Right at this moment, she noticed, Helga's eyes were flickering in great interest from Jamie to Dominic and back again. There was a certain, faraway smile on her face ...

'Oh. My ID.' Helga remembered. She undraped her arm from Coco and stood up, flashing a bright smile at Dominic as she did so. He was leaning against a cupboard, drinking beer; thoughts which had no relation to cocaine smuggling were beginning to stir in the aristocratic Englishman's mind. His friend Jamie had the welcome habit of getting them into libidinous situations. Unless he was very much mistaken, this little meeting had all the promise of developing into one of those ...

From her bag, Helga produced a Hong Kong police department card with her photograph on it. She passed it to Jamie, who treated it to a most cursory glance and handed it back. His mind, too, was drifting to other things as he recollected Coco's well-striped backside on the beach yesterday, appreciating that this German policewoman had been the one to inflict that punishment; on Queenie, too. The girls' little bruises and fading red welts would endure for at least another week.

'Yeah, fine Helga,' he said. 'Thanks.' His eyes ran slowly up and down the sexily clad, statuesque body, amazed that it was controlled by the brain of a policewoman, speculating, wondering ...

As for Helga – Helga was Helga. A sexual sixth sense picked up these impure thoughts hovering in the air of

146

her cabin, and she decided that if they did not shortly crystallise into action of their own accord then she would need to do something about it. Jamie she had had her eye on ever since the trip began. The Englishman looked most interesting. Aristocrats, she had long since discovered, tended towards the eccentric in matters carnal . . .

'You have the most amazing gear in there,' said Jamie, with a nod towards the cupboard which Dominic leant against.

'I already forgave your prying.' Helga returned to the bed where she sat and dropped her arm once more around Coco's shoulders. 'So you stuck your nose in my things? Pretty kinky stuff, collected the world over. Rubber, leather, silks, satins, I got the lot. Which is it you prefer, Jamie?'

'Me, I dig just about anything feminine,' said Jamie easily. 'If it's a bit kinky, even better.'

Helga's green eyes danced in amusement from Jamie to Dominic. 'You, too, no, I bet?' she said. 'Want to take look in there?'

'All right,' said Dominic. The scene was very definitely setting, as it were. He opened the wardrobe drawer to come face to face with Helga's leather outerwear: two dozen different items hanging tightly packed together.

'Rubber in the two top drawers – stockings, bras and corsets. Other skin gear lower down,' chanted Helga, as if she were the lift attendant in a department store.

Dominic briefly glanced inside the top drawer. He took out a pair of pink rubber, crotchless panties, examined them, held them up for all to see, then put them back, closing the drawer. 'I'll take your word for the rest,' he said. 'Not quite the done thing, is it? A gentleman rummaging through a lady's underwear?'

'Rummage – a splendid word, no?' said Helga. 'I enjoy rummaging through Coco's underwear, especially when she's wearing it, don't I, darling?' Her hand slipped under Coco's dress, travelling two-thirds of the way up her thigh, and she drew them closer together, tenderly kissing her.

While she gladly let this happen to her, Coco covertly

147

watched Jamie and Dominic; both of them went quiet and still, eyes trapped by this occurrence. Coco, aware that a little lesbian exhibitionism is guaranteed to turn most men on very quickly, responded to Helga's advance with passion, her tongue toying with the German's as her eyes sexily hooked Jamie's.

After watching this embrace for perhaps a minute, Jamie protested, 'Heh, don't hog the kid to yourself, Helga. Coco's my girl.'

Helga broke off the kiss. Her hand crept to the top of Coco's warm thigh, green fingernails resting lightly at the crotch of her panties. 'Your girl?' she echoed. 'How so? She is in my arms – you will have to take her away from me!'

'We're lovers, you know that,' teased Coco. 'You'll never guess how we did it yesterday.' She brushed her lips against Helga's ear, still watching Jamie. 'On a horse,' she whispered.

'On a horse?' exclaimed Helga. 'But how is this so? This must have been a most quiet animal, no?'

'The horse was running.'

'I've now heard the lot,' said Dominic, moving away from the wardrobe. 'Am I to understand that you two had sex on a galloping horse?'

'Mmmm. It was sensational. He did it with Queenie first, at a trot. Then with me at full gallop!'

'Let's gallop some more,' said Jamie with quiet force. 'Sorry, Helga, I will take her away from you. I don't go for Nick – he just ain't my type!' Taking hold of Coco by her bare elbow, he pulled her up and off the bed, Helga's hand sliding reluctantly down and off her leg. As he took Coco in his arms, Jamie said, 'How about a little music, Helga? Let's dance some.'

Dancing, Jamie had figured, was probably the quickest way to get Dominic and Helga together, though he had his doubts as to how this oddball female would respond with a man. With Jamie already shuffling Coco around in his arms, Helga selected the soft music channel, and closed the curtains over the portholes. Then she opened her arms wide in welcome and walked straight into Dominic's.

Instant sex. No muttered, casual words. No slow getting accustomed to strange body being close to strange body. No dancing, even. Helga ground her hips into Dominic as if he was the man she had been waiting for all of her life. Raising her hands, she cupped his face between them, crushing her mouth on to his and kissed him with fiery passion. Dominic, momentarily taken aback by the onslaught, took only seconds to respond. His cock began to stir as his pelvis and tongue went into action.

Jamie and Coco danced for a while, kissing, as Dominic and Helga toppled over together on to the bed. It was a softly swaying dance of the utmost carnality, Jamie's hand finding its unstoppable way under the elastic back of the top of Coco's skirt, into the silken panties, and on down between hot, bare buttocks to finger her pussy as her hand slid palm forwards between her belly and his jeans to encourage the bulge beneath them to further hardness. They crept slowly around the cabin, locked in their kiss and their groping and their rising priapic tide.

Helga has an unprotesting Dominic pinned to the bed. She kneels over him, her weight on his wrists which are flattened on either side of his shoulders, the scarlet, kid crotch of her culottes sliding up and down over the zipper area of his slacks, bringing his penis to full erection. 'It would perhaps bring pleasure to you if I whip you a little – nothing too painful, you understand?' she mutters in her throatiest imitation of Marlene Dietrich.

Dominic, who in fact would not mind that at all, declines; this is not something he cares to let himself be subjected to with his macho pal a witness.

Her crotch rhythmically rotating, Helga murmurs regretfully, 'Very well. This is a pity, because I am a specialist, you see. But you will oblige me with a slight beating later?'

'Maybe.'

'Good. Now, lie very still.' She slides down his body until her nose is hovering over his zipper, which she swiftly opens. She undoes the top button of his trousers and pulls them down his thighs, dragging yellow mini-slips after them. For once the Honourable Dominic, gazing in rapt fascination as the high-coiffured blonde head ducks into his genitals, spares no thought for his immaculate cream slacks. She has a most refined and practised way with her mouth, this bisexual beauty. Drawing in her cheeks, she curls the edges of her tongue upwards on the underside of his erection, getting his penis wet, sucking air through her lips and over it, making it delightfully cool as the tips of the fingers of both her hands grasp his testicles and twist them, as if she is twiddling knobs.

Her attention lasciviously attracted by Helga's actions, whilst submitting gratefully to Jamie's plunging fingers beneath her knickers, Coco unzips the master of the *Star of Kowloon*. As they shuffle-dance on, she fishes inside his jeans and hauls out his warm, solid cock, fisting it straight up against her belly between them, and lazily masturbating it in that commodious attitude to the raunchily deep sounds of Nina Simone's 'Who Wants a Little Sugar in Her Bowl'.

Two decks below this fast heating-up, four-sided orgy, the blackest of male buttocks are heaving and pumping away, with Queenie's feet, dusty on their bottoms, crossed over them, heavy black testicles thumping into her each time Bobo's cock reaches the depth of her vagina.

A high-pitched, piping sound intrudes on their sexual bliss.

'Oh, shit!' exclaims the engineer with a glance at the wall-clock. 'Time to start her up, fuck it!' Reaching behind himself he opens Queenie's feet off him, heaves himself to his knees on the bed, then climbs down to the deck, big erection slickly glistening. 'Sorry, honey,' he mutters. 'Work to do. But don't you even think of leaving!'

He mutters something – unintelligible to Queenie – into a tube affair on the bulkhead. Beginning to slip from the very edge of orgasm, feeling drastically let down, she watches him stride naked out of the cabin and into the engine room, leaving the metal door slightly ajar.

A slight shudder runs through the ship, then another, as the engines roar into life before settling into a barely discernible throb. By now Jamie is minus his Levis – as

Coco, holding her skirt above her hips, his fingers hooking the crotch of her knickers out of the way, her back to him, lowers her pussy to his waiting erection. Jamie, like Bobo, has understandably lost all track of time.

'Hell!' he grunts. 'We're putting to sea. I should be on the fucking bridge.'

His glans in intimate contact with her vulva, beginning to sink into it, he flattens his hands behind her thighs and pushes her bottom up and away. 'You're not serious?' she gasps, as he lifts her leg up and slides out from under her.

'As master, I'm expected to be with my Captain when we sail. I've gotta go.' He grins fleetingly at her as he retrieves his jeans from the deck and begins to clumsily climb into them. Coco turns around and sinks into the armchair, staring at him in frustrated astonishment. He nods at his hard-on as he crams the denim over it, and pulls up his zip with difficulty. 'You don't have any tricks to get this down, do you?' he says.

'Try a bucket of cold water,' mutters Coco, peeved. 'It works for dogs. Jesus Christ!'

'Look, I'll be fifteen minutes, okay?' He glances at the bed where Dominic, paying scant notice of him, is at last putting his trousers into their creases, while Helga slips out of her culottes. 'Watch them and play with yourself until I get back!'

Below, Queenie has come to terms with the interruption. Feeling overwhelmingly horny, she sneaks naked from the engineer's cabin, bare feet encounting the cold steel of the engine-room deck as her eyes fall on Bobo's muscular rear. He is bending over a dial in his maze of powerful machinery, studying a reading. She creeps up on him, and he freezes as she curves both hands over his heavy buttocks.

The *Star of Kowloon* begins to move.

'Lady, I'm checking the engines,' he says, not turning around.

One of her hands slips over his belly and down through his pubic hairs, to find his slightly drooping erection. 'And I'm checking yours!' she responds, jerking on it.

'You are some raver, aren't you?' he mumbles as, still not looking at her, he adjusts something, letting her hand rest where it is.

'I'm a cabin girl,' she mutters, pleased to feel his cock rapidly thicken to full dimensions as she rubs it. 'Personal assistant to the Chief Engineer. How'm I doing?'

Just about everthing seems to be vibrating in this huge engine room, even the floor under their feet. There is a feeling of raw power all around them. In being nude here with this handsome black man, in masturbating him as he fiddles with the controls of such power. Queenie discovers an unimaginable kick.

'You're doin' just fine, ma'am,' he declares as he makes a final adjustment and turns around. 'Back to the sack.'

But Queenie has other ideas. She drops to her knees on the hard steel, looks up at him with pleading, doey eyes and mutters, 'Let's fuck right here?' – before fisting his cock into her mouth. He grunts, jerks his hips. With her eyes fixed on his, she unmouths him and says, 'Please, mister. Please?'

He glances at his hands, which are soiled with grease. 'Whatever turns you on,' he says thickly. 'First let me clean these.'

She stands, trailing her breasts slowly up over his hard-on as she does so. Then she takes both his hands in hers and turns them palms upwards, staring at them. 'Wipe them off on my tits,' she murmurs wickedly. 'I think I'd enjoy that. I'm feeling very dirty!'

'You're a nutter, Queenie.' But he evidently likes this idea himself, because he does not hesitate. His greasy hands close over her breasts, engulfing them, smearing brown engine oil over the freckles as she squirms in delight. The head of his cock prods her navel.

Queenie's lust-filled eyes fall on the rail which guards a part of the engine where pistons pound away. It is cold, gleaming chrome and it trembles with a life of its own. Moving away from Bobo, trailing a white smear through her soiled breasts with a finger, and putting a dab of grease on her belly with it, she goes to the rail, grips it

152

with her hands at hip height, and doubles herself across it, muttering, 'Come on, Bobo, give it to your cabin girl. Do me!'

Fires rage through him, out of control. He had had some hot female flesh in his time, but no one quite as rampant as Queenie. He can't wait to once again get it up this beautiful raver. Making no sound beyond a single, massive grunt, the naked Zulu Indian positions himself behind Queenie, lowering slightly at the knees, swoops his hands around the front of her thighs and into the heart of their softness, finds her vulva lips with his fingers and pulls them apart. He manoeuvres his glans between them without need to steer it with a hand, and shoves, sliding easily up to the root, as Queenie sucks in air through clenched teeth and closes her eyes.

Bobo fucks Queenie, not with the steady rhythm of the pistons below them, but massively, withdrawing his penis to the glans, pausing, then banging it into her for all he is worth, pausing, withdrawing, banging again, his bulging, straining thigh muscles slapping into the back of her legs, his balls flying forwards between them with each pound as she quivers and gasps and moans.

Cold chromed steel is vibrating through Queenie's desperately clutching hands and into her belly and upper thighs. The steel under her bare feet shivers with the motors, and everything is alive. She opens her tortured eyes on the powerful pistons, her gaze roves a little crazily over the throbbing engines as her belly and thighs are rammed into the rail and her tits rock violently with each relentless thrust. She looks wildly down under her own body, between her bouncing breasts and beneath the rail, her eyes fixing on the swollen, black testicles as they ride, and jiggle and bounce to and fro. And Queenie, Lady Granville – down in the bowels of this floating casino without a single pillow or cushion to comfort her, surrounded by pitiless steel – is in paradise.

Chief Engineer Bobo is building up to what will be one of the most memorable climaxes of his life. Queenie feels this, her own orgasm is rushing up on her, but she has a yen to be even closer to the living steel when it happens. 'On the deck,' she gasps. 'Quickly, lover, quickly. Fuck me on my back, right here.'

Silently, restraining orgasm only just, he uncouples. Queenie prostrates herself at his feet, knees bent, thighs parted – the jogging steel cold and hard beneath her buttocks and shoulderblades, like some mammoth slow-motion vibrator. Her eyes are fixed on Bobo's penis as he kneels between her legs, taking his weight on hands and knees, and lowers his groin to hers. His cock fails to find its way home as easily as it did from behind, so she helps it, eyes leching on the sight, her vagina contracting as it sinks into her until their pubic hairs, red and black, mingle.

The immense power of the ship trembles all through Queenie's body, transmitted via the throbbing metal at her back. It combines with the strength of the rutting male who no longer pauses with each thrust, but now matches the pounding of the pistons, the entire fucking motion performed with hips alone. His knees are hurting against the deck, but he barely notices this as he fucks, and fucks, and fucks, until his semen pours into her like lava from an exploding volcano. He roars mightily with his orgasm, the noise drowning Queenie's scream, and his hips go through a diminishingly violent series of shudders until his balls are empty. Then he sags on to his elbows, heavily panting, head lolling, body still.

Queenie, enormously content, remains finely tuned to the steady trembling of the steel deck at her back, one living half of a sexual sandwich which will pound on in her memory for ever.

Bobo gradually becomes aware of some pain and of slight cramps in knees and elbows. He climbs awkwardly to his feet, a kneecap cracking. Taking Queenie by the hand he pulls her to a sitting position and helps her to her feet. His eyes laze over her grease-smeared breasts and smudged belly, then gaze languidly into hers. Amazingly, somewhere in their inky depths she detects a spark of yet unkindled lust.

'I hurt,' he says with a wry grin. 'Let's go lay down on the bed.'

Jamie was let into Helga's cabin by Coco, who was wearing nothing but a frilly little blouse. As she closed the door behind him and locked it she said, her eyes hovering in the region of his groin, 'Got it down yet?' She smirked at him insinuatingly.

He most certainly had, but the sight of her half-naked display brought him an immediate stirring. He stared from her rose tattoo to the bed where Helga, stripped to boots, black stockings and a thin red rubber corset, was riding the nude Dominic, her hips jerking in exactly the same fashion as they did when she was performing with her dildo; like those of a love-making man. They were too engrossed in their copulation to take more than a second's notice of Jamie's entrance.

Coco cast lascivious eyes on them. 'Helga fucking a man,' she murmured. 'Amazing what can happen in just a quarter of an hour.' She flattened her hand over the crotch of Jamie's jeans, and sensuously rubbed the inside of her thigh against the outside of his. 'Could we maybe get back to where we left off?' she pleaded. 'I'm horny as hell!'

The combination of the sight of Helga's heaving, rounded buttocks and her vagina sliding vigorously up and down Dominic's shaft, and Coco's hot little hand pressing on his penis through his jeans, brings Jamie an immediate erection. He unzips himself and takes out his cock, putting it in Coco's palm.

'So, exactly where were we?' he mutters.

Moments later, Coco is sitting astride Jamie in the armchair, her back to him, hands planted by his thighs, jammed into the sides of the chair. He is still wearing his opened jeans and Coco is doing to him what Helga is doing to Dominic, their lust fed by the sight of Helga's bouncing behind. With her feet planted on the carpet, Coco bobs her fine little behind up and down as if it is perched atop a fast-trotting horse with a dildo fixed to the saddle. Her eyes switch to and fro from ogling the action on the bed to her own penetration. Jamie's hands are up under the front of Coco's blouse, cupping her breasts, rolling her erect nipples between fingers and thumbs as her buttocks jump faster, slapping down on to his thighs while she makes mewling noises which grow steadily louder.

Orgasm comes speedily to Jamie and Coco; the interruption has been lengthy, the stimulation is considerable. As he begins to flood into her, Coco raises herself off him. She curves her fingers around the back of his ejaculating penis, stoops over it and directs the semen over her breasts and belly. Feeling totally, deliciously wanton in this action, she lets his cock go and smears the sperm into her flesh with circling motions of her palm, as a few final drops spill on to the carpet. Then her buttocks bump their way between Jamie's thighs, she slips through his knees and sinks to the floor, her back resting against the chair between his spread legs – her glazed, wilful, happy eyes still on Helga's backside, which continues to grind and heave on top of Dominic.

The English aristocrat and the German lesbian are proving to be surprisingly well tuned sexually. Helga has done most of the work from the beginning, riding the two of them on the crest of the sort of carnal wave which can sweep on indefinitely without carrying them uncontrollably to orgasm. But eventually Helga wants something different, this business of straight sex contents her only for a limited amount of time. 'Whip me a little?' she suddenly whispers into Dominic's ear, her hips giving an extra powerful surge as the notion adds to her excitement. 'Whip my bum?'

'Sure,' agrees Dominic, with an amused, cynical smile.

She climbs off his penis, strides in her boots past the resting Jamie and Coco, with barely a glance at them, and fetches her riding crop.

Sitting up on the bed, hard-on pointing into a corner of the cabin, Dominic takes the crop and flexes it. But it scares him a little, this steel-cored, plaited leather instrument. He realises that, over-enthusiastically administered, it could be a dangerous weapon, and he has no intention of inflicting injury on Helga – even if Helga goes for it. 'No,' he says. He drops the crop on the bed. Reaching for his trousers he slides the thin, crocodile belt from its loops. 'This.' His eyes narrowed.

'*Ja*,' agrees Helga, eyes shining. '*Ist gut*.' She kneels on the bed, naked bottom raised in offering, forearms flat on the cover to form a V, hands joined, cheek resting on them. She wiggles her hips provocatively. 'Hard. Do it hard,' she insists.

This Dominic goes for in a big way. He wants to lay into her with some force, he loves a bit of this stuff now and again, so long as it does no great damage; a thrashing with the thin belt will merely stripe her, but the crop brought down on her with equal force would cut deep into her flesh.

As the other two, rapidly awakening to what is about to happen, stare intrigued, naked, rampant Dominic raises his belt-hand high behind his shoulder, and brings the crocodile hide down with stinging strength across Helga's eagerly awaiting buttocks.

'Oh, *jaaa!*' she moans as it thwacks into them. She wriggles her butt. 'More,' she pleads. 'Much, much more!' Dominic obligingly raises his arm.

As the belt slaps into her bottom again and again with stinging force, Dominic's solid penis trembling at each blow, Helga's hand steals beneath her, her fingers find her clitoris, and she begins to masturbate faster and faster as her quivering buttocks turn rosy – criss-crossed with thick red welts.

After giving Helga more than a dozen blows, Dominic can hold back from penetration no longer. His lust is enflamed to bursting point by the sight of what he has inflicted. Dropping the belt, he climbs up on the bed on his knees behind Helga, slips his cock into her, and with a few massive heaves of his hips – which bring animal grunts to the German's lips – he shoots his sperm into her as she brings herself off with her fingertips. In slow motion, Helga collapses forward on the bed, Dominic going with her until she is flat on her face, with him lying on her back, penis beginning to wilt within her.

'Jesus,' remarked Jamie, 'that turned the kinky bastard on like nobody's business!' He was clearly astounded by what he had witnessed. 'What a fucking combination – Nick with his aristocratic English weirdo stuff and a Teutonic Amazon with a taste for S and M. Beats me!'

He was not aware of it, since he could only see the back of her head, her shoulders and her lower legs, but Coco, whose reaction to the thrashing had been singularly different from his own, had two fingers stuck up inside herself and was slowly moving them. She twisted her head to look at him with a languid smile. 'You're too conventional by half, baby!' she remarked.

'Conventional?' Jamie exclaimed blankly. 'What, me?'

As the ship steamed out into its waters, the Gulf of Manila was placid, in contrast to the activities aboard which, between hot gambling and even hotter sex, were almost enough to rock the boat. Queenie was indulging herself in an afternoon to remember for the rest of her life, strenuous, fulfilling, almost non-stop sex which would appear later as scorching little enigmatic notes in her diary. Having briefly interrupted their renewed copulation to check something in his engine room, Bobo now literally leapt back on to her on the bed, with the enthusiasm of a sweating man diving into the ship's pool. Impaling her to the hilt, he then lay on top of her, rocking his hips in a slow, lazy dance. A man whose initial, frenetic passion is spent can afford to take his time.

Bobo, his hands screwed into fists on either side of Queenie's shoulders, his thumbs touching them, gazes down wonderingly into her eyes. 'I still don't believe you,' he mutters.

Her dimple cracks prettily. She feels wondrously content and comfortable with this ongoing fuck, her pussy a warm, smooth, spoiled sheath – the very centre of her existence. 'How on earth did a Zulu Indian ever get made?' she ventures.

'Oh, pretty well like this,' he tells her with a smile, his easy rhythm unchanging.

She produces a deep-throated laugh. 'It would be quite some baby, yours and mine!'

The atmosphere in Helga's cabin is a heavy blanket of lust. The four of them have reached a stage in their orgy where each one is aware that its prolonging is inevitable, that further libidinous pleasures are just around the corner. They are all wallowing in a hedonistic, carnal luxury akin to the middle part of some bacchanalian feast where the revellers eagerly await the next goblet of heady wine, another bunch of juicy, luscious grapes.

Helga and Dominic are sprawled together on the sofa, legs entwined, Helga has Dominic's limp penis in her hand, and idly plays with it. Coco lazes on Jamie's lap in the armchair, as Jamie toys with her nipple.

Breaking the heavy silence, Helga says gruffly, 'You know what I should enjoy next, Coco darling?'

'Surprise me,' says Coco.

'I believe it is true when I say this will be a very special kick for the two of us.'

'No more riding crop, huh?' Coco wriggles. 'My butt isn't recovered from the last time!'

'Crop, no.' Helga purses her lips. 'How would you like to try out my dildo – on me?'

Coco's features crease in an amused, prurient grin. 'I never did that,' she says. 'Yeah, why not?'

Jamie, who was gently tracing the outline of Coco's rose tattoo with his finger, muttered, 'you're going to use a dildo on her?' His finger stilled. 'Christ, what next?'

'Like I said, why not?'

On the music system, Sinatra was Wrapping his Troubles in Dreams as Helga paid a visit to her kinkiest drawer and produced from it her pink rubber dildo. 'Get up,' she said to Coco. 'I fix it.'

Coco stood. Dominic looked on in lustful amusement, Jamie in lusty puzzlement, as Helga knelt in front of Coco. 'You are wet, no?' she asked her.

'You'd better believe it.'

'This is good.' Spreading Coco's labia with two fingers, Helga plugged her with the extension on the back of the dildo. 'You hold on to it,' she instructed. 'I will tie the straps tight, as they should be.'

With her fingers gripping the shaft of the plastic phallus, the hairs of her lush, black bush overlapping its base, feeling both slightly stupid and extremely ribald, Coco waited while Helga adjusted the tiny buckles on the velvet harness, one of the straps biting gently, deep between her buttocks. When the dildo was in place, the German rocked back on her heels and admired it, saying, 'You can let go of it now. Let us all see how you look.'

The dildo stood out in front of Coco at just above forty-five degrees, its angled back end stuck very firmly up her, the tiny sheath for her clitoris comfortably in position. Gazing down at this sight made Coco feel very odd, yet amazingly dirty.

'Coco, the clown!' Jamie ventured, laughing. He was ignored.

'Wank it a bit. You will see how nice,' breathed Helga.

With a tiny smirk on her lips, challenging Jamie with insolent eyes, she did just that; the action felt silly, but the end jiggling inside her and the motion of the clitoris extension were pleasantly arousing. Jamie's expression came close to mocking her whilst Dominic's was undiluted lust as he handled his growing penis.

'Ja,' muttered Helga in satisfaction. 'Ja, ja.' She got to her feet, fondled Coco's breasts for a moment, then unbuttoned her blouse and slipped it off, throwing it over a chair. 'Come.' Taking Coco's hand she led her to the bed. 'Please, Dominic, some room?' she suggested. The Englishman rolled himself tight against the bulkhead.

Helga sat down, swung her legs up and lay on her back, spreading her black-stockinged, black-booted legs and reaching her arms towards Coco, who stood at the foot of the bed, a hand wrapped around the dildo, savouring this pre-penetration moment as she tried to make up her mind what her emotions were. Her experiences of lesbian sex –

apart from being entered by this self-same dildo – had always been unaccompanied by artificial aids. She decided she was keen for this new experience, as Helga commanded, 'Come,' her fingers hooking in impatient little jerks. '*Fick* me!'

Coco's knees indented the bottom of the bed. She dropped to her elbows on either side of Helga's thighs and walked them towards her shoulders, until the two women were belly to belly, breasts crushed against breasts. Reaching between their legs, Helga slipped the end of the dildo inside her; Coco had no idea it was in place until the German commanded. 'Push!' Coco rocked her hips until their pubic hairs enmeshed. '*Fick* me, *fick* me!' grated Helga. 'You must pretend that you are a man.'

Quickly getting the hang of this new form of carnality, Coco soon found herself wallowing in it. The difference, for her, between a naked, pubis-to-pubis lesbian encounter and this was the all-important stimulating effect of the ingenious extensions to the dildo. She found that, with her hand between them and her fingers resting in Helga's bush, tips of two touching the sliding plastic, she could judge when she had almost withdrawn from Helga, plunging once more at exactly the right moment. She established much the same rhythm as she had whilst impaled on Jamie on the armchair, bottom happily jerking while she licked and nibbled Helga's ear.

Jamie's facetiousness had drowned in lust as he watched. Like Dominic, he had a full hard-on once more and he dwelt hungrily on Coco's lustily rocking buttocks with hooded eyes.

The ladies roll on to their sides, the better to play with each other's breasts and to kiss and caress as the lesbian fuck hots up. Dominic, his back crushed into the bulkhead, finds his erection repeatedly banged by Coco's warm, thrusting rear end.

The scene progresses towards a climax of unrivalled bawdiness.

Finding these writhing sensuous buttocks with their red velvet strap and their continuous knocking into him,

161

irresistible, Dominic begs Coco to stay still for a moment. He pulls the strap and the base of the dildo to one side, and eases the head of his cock in to Coco's pussy while Helga, not about to be brought down from her rising high, does the hip-jerking.

Little by little, as Coco gasps and moans, Dominic slides his cock deep into her. When it is up as far as it will go, he grunts into Coco's ear, 'Right. Do the lady some more.' Coco's nubile buttocks begin to rock as she plunges the dildo in and out of Helga.

Jamie stands over the bed, hard-on throbbing through his open jeans, looking down on this Rabelaisian performance with leching eyes. Many a man would have pleasured himself with masturbation at this point, but the Australian, except in extreme situations, is not the onanistic type. He needs penetration. Pussy or painted lips will fit the bill, but he craves penetration now.

Helga's thighs are wrapped around Coco's, one of them underneath hers, her big white bum, in its rubber-corset frame, sways and rocks, protruding invitingly over the edge of the narrow bed.

Decided, and once decided unable to resist his course of action, Jamie climbs out of his jeans. Piling cushions on the deck he kneels on them. Seconds later, making her go almost still and bite her lip with the initial stretching of it, his huge cock is cramming itself up beside the dildo.

The German has been this road before – Helga has travelled almost every imaginable route – but only with a man attached to the other penis, not a darling oriental girl. She very quickly gets comfortable in her sandwich and begins to purr in delight, not as a cat might, but like a tigress.

The extraordinary four-way fuck gets into its stride, the women having the best of both worlds, Coco going wild, twisting Helga's breasts almost savagely which the German, naturally, minds not in the least. Coco is lost in the double ecstasy of her lesbian assault on Helga, and, perhaps best of all, Dominic's penetration, which her writhing hips give most of the movement to. All Dominic needs do, apart from barely rocking his pelvis through more than half an inch or so, is see to it that his penis stays in place.

This is group sex at its most salacious, a sweaty, rapacious mingling of bodies with minds functioning at their most primitive levels, an experience sending lightning bolts of ecstasy through all four of them and bringing them together as a single, ravenous, carnal beast which climaxes with shudder after shudder surging through its flesh and with gasp after gasp on its four, slavering mouths.

After long minutes of panting silence, Coco, on her back, her thigh crushing Dominic's flaccid penis, her own plastic one pointing rigidly at the underside of the deck above them, lets loose a heavy sigh of replete contentment and opens her eyes. Her hand falls on the dildo, gripping it. She smiles. For anyone who cares to listen, she mutters, 'Bingo! I guess there can't be much left after that, can there?'

# 10

## Saved by The Belle

Despite grave fears to the contrary, the three days spent cruising around South Luzon, stopping off at the Island of Marinduque and at Magnog, passed without any physical threat to Queenie or Coco or Helga. There were some pleasant, one-to-one sexual meetings, but nothing even vaguely approaching the dissoluteness of that afternoon in Helga's cabin in the Gulf of Manila.

The girls got on with their job of wrapping up their notes and photos in preparation for the final article for *Madame*, whilst taking every precaution with their persons. Their guns were always ready and handy in their suite, the outer cabin door double locked. They slept with the stateroom door propped wide open so that they might hear any attempt at forcing the outer door. That was perhaps just as well, since on the night after steaming out of Magnog, Queenie, asleep in Coco's arms, was awoken by the sounds of a key rattling in the lock and a scraping noise on the door. Acting foolishly bravely, she went to it naked, gun in hand, shot the bolt and opened it – by which time whoever had been there had vanished. But the attempt was confirmation, as if it were needed, that they were still in danger.

No more than two kilometres square, the provincial city of Legaspi was overshadowed by the frequently active volcano of Mayon, two and a half thousand metres high and awe-inspiringly beautiful, reputed to be the world's most perfectly shaped volcano.

Masters and Li were amongst the first to disembark, almost as soon as the ship had docked in the small harbour. Helga was close behind them, keeping them in sight whilst most careful not to be spotted by them herself. Despite the city's small size and the fact that Queenie and Coco spent half the day wandering around and exploring there, and having lunch, they never bumped into any one of the three.

Trouble with a capital T did not descend until the *Star of Kowloon* had left Legaspi and was heading north once more in Laganoy Gulf, on the final leg of its voyage.

'I was kinda having these exciting visions of bumping into you,' said Luk, to Coco, who was playing blackjack.

The contrary could be said for Coco who, in consideration of Luk's connection with Masters, had been making great efforts to avoid the Chinese girl. Sitting next to Coco, Luk ordered some chips. She wore another of her cheongsams, this one in shiny peach silk with embossed dragons, slit to the top of the thigh which was perched next to Coco's, and she smelt of a musky, exotic perfume.

'You were?' Coco responded. 'That's nice. How ya been?' Her eyes stayed on the cards as she watched the dealer hit her twelve with the King of Diamonds and bust her.

'Okay, I guess.' Luk sighed. 'Life can be a bit of a drag with that fuckin' Masters.' She placed a heavy bet and drew a six and a five. 'But the bread more or less makes up for it.' She doubled her bet. 'Hit me, honey – don't hurt me.'

Coco kept her eyes down. 'At least he hasn't threatened to kill you yet,' she said, staying on fifteen after Luk drew a ten. The dealer, for a change, went over the top.

'One of these days, Coco.' She giggled. 'I ain't never gonna forget the way you threw him. Too fuckin' much!'

'Yeah. He hit the deck like a great sack of lard, didn't he?' Coco watched the dealer's hands, fast, slim and elegant with nicely manicured silver nails, as she said, 'So why were you looking for me?'

'Kinda looking for you.' Luk shifted her bare knee so that it was touching Coco's lower thigh. Coco, wearing a pair of very short, tight hot pants, felt a tingle of excitement run up her leg at the contact. 'Like I said, Masters bores the shit out of me, y'know?' She slid Coco a sideways look, slanty eyes rapidly travelling over Coco's loose, well-filled T-shirt which had a huge head of Marilyn Monroe on its front. 'I prefer girls.' Saying this, she shifted her leg still further so that both their thighs were touching. 'You know that.'

A lump formed in Coco's throat as she remembered the last time with its doubly ignominious ending. Certainly it had been fun for a while on that massively stormy sea, but it had never been properly consummated. Had it not been for the confrontation with Masters they would surely have found one another's arms since then. Despite her misgivings about further dalliance with Masters' whore, she returned the pressure of the leg. 'Yeah.' For the first time since the Chinese girl had perched beside her, Coco turned her eyes on her. 'I know that all right.'

'It's been a long time. A whole week, doll.'

'Yeah.'

'There are still two hours before dinner.' Luk dropped her hand on Coco's knee.

Swallowing, Coco said, 'Listen, Luk, you know damn well that me and my girlfriend are in a certain amount of trouble with Masters.' She paused, 'And with Li.'

Luk shrugged. 'So you dumped Masters on his fat arse. Serve him right; he shouldn't have gone for you. And so what? He ain't done nothing to get back at you.'

'There's a whole lot more to it than that.'

Infinitely slowly, walking the fingers, Luk moved a hand up Coco's thigh, until the little finger was touching the edge of her shorts. 'Nothing that I know about, honey. I take the bread, do my bit for it, and stick around. But I keep my peepers and shell pinks strictly closed. I seriously don't want to know.'

Enormously tempted by this promise of imminent, heavenly, soft and gentle sex with this sensuous girl, Coco persuaded herself to believe her. As Luk squeezed her thigh, she locked eyes with hers, cards and latest lost bet forgotten, fresh stake unplaced. Nevertheless, shaking her head, hair brushing over her back as the lump in her throat slipped down to her belly, she muttered, 'I, I dunno.'

But Luk merely smiled, and increased the pressure on her thigh. 'We won't go to my cabin, of course. We'll go to yours, huh?'

Coco gave in. Unable to resist the delectable temptation, she murmured, 'Let's do that,' and slipped from her stool.

As they made their way quickly through the casino throng, Coco caught a warning frown from Queenie, who was interviewing someone as he played roulette. But Coco was too far into what was about to happen to take the slightest notice.

On slightly spread knees, facing one another on the bed, Coco and Luk, eyes shining with the sheer wonderment of what they are doing, fondle each other with both hands, touching and exploring as if this is the first time for them. Indeed, Coco is so taken with the Chinese girl that she actually is reliving the same depths of emotional and sexual discovery which accompanied her first ever lesbian love-making.

The *Star of Kowloon* is riding a soft swell in the Gulf, creaking easily and gently from port to starboard and back again, just enough to rock the two girls as if they are in a giant, comforting cradle. With Coco's hand within the slit of her cheongsam, curled around the inside top of her warm thigh, the side of the knuckle of her index finger digging into the soft wetness beneath lace knickers and gentling back and forth there between the labia, Luk takes hold of Coco's Marilyn T-shirt and tugs it free of her shorts. Coco's breasts tremble engagingly beneath the smile of Miss Monroe. Luk slides her hands, palms flat, fingers upwards, thumbs touching, up over Coco's taut belly to her breasts, where she lets them rest, rolling them very slightly, hard nipples pressing into her palms.

Coco's spare hand steals behind Luk's neck, under the

short black hair, and she pulls their lips together. It is a long, lingering, most tender kiss, just the very tips of their tongues touching and flickering over each other, and, during it, one of Luk's hands drifts back down over Coco's belly to find, through her shorts, her pussy, in the same fashion that Coco's has found hers with the side of the index finger. The kiss goes on and on, the fingers gently probe, passions rise as juices flow, and they mumble words of sex into one another's mouths.

Coco's finger works its way under Luk's panties and slips into her tight, damp little hole as Luk, eager for similar intimate contact, unzips Coco's shorts and pulls them, and her knickers, down to her knees. She hooks two fingers into Coco's vagina, up to the knuckles. Locked together in this most intimate of carnal caresses, tongues mingling deeper and faster within their mouths, they bring each other steadily towards a peak of pleasure.

Her interview with the pedantic Middle-western American cattle rancher at an end, Queenie realised that she was experiencing disconcerting stirrings of worry over the fact that Coco had gone off somewhere with Luk. She put the cassette-recorder in her bag and left the roulette table, hurrying for the casino exit.

A bulky Chinaman, in a dark blue silk suit and a colourful tie, watched her progress until she was almost at the door, then went after her, beckoning to another, smaller oriental. This man followed him until they reached a companionway, then he darted through the ship to the next set of stairs.

Taking scant notice of the oriental who approached her, as she paused outside her cabin, fishing in her bag for her key, Queenie was unaware that the man in the blue silk suit was now stealthily closing in on her from behind.

As her key slid into the lock, Queenie looked up in surprise into his grinning face as the smaller man said, 'Excuse, lady?'

'Yes?' she said. She sensed too late that something was seriously amiss when she heard the ripping sound of sticky tape behind her. She started to turn her head. As the big Chinaman came into view, a six-centimetre-wide band of brown tape was yanked around her mouth; the other man grabbed her hand from the key and opened the door.

Unable to produce a sound beyond a muffled scream into the tape, Queenie tried to run, but her hands were gripped behind her and she was shoved into the cabin. Saying not a word, the two men went in after her, and one quietly closed the door. Similar tape as that used to gag her was now employed to bind her hands tightly behind her back. Her eyes blazing terror, she suddenly felt very, very sick.

Coco, desperate for the warmth and sensuality of a naked embrace, was fumbling Luk out of her cheongsam. She heard not a thing.

Trembling in fear, Queenie was violently shoved back into a chair. The men made no sound, their expressions said nothing. Dropping to his haunches, the big one removed Queenie's shoes. As his meaty fingers found the zip in her knee-length skirt, the thought that this was to be a rape added to her terror. But, as he dragged the skirt down over her legs, she realised that at least rape would not be as bad a fate as if these were Masters' men come to kill her.

She sat, unable to resist, trembling from head to toe, fighting back an urge to vomit, as her knickers joined the skirt and shoes on the carpet. The watching oriental's face was most certainly not without expression at this stage; it was twisted with lust as the buttons down the front of her blouse were ripped undone and her breasts swung free.

But, then, from the inside pocket of his jacket, the hulk produced a flick-knife, pressed its button and the gleaming blade sprang open. He was going to kill her! Queenie went faint with engulfing terror as the knife moved towards her.

But he used the weapon only to slit through the short sleeves of her blouse, so that he could pull it off her while her hands were tied. Finally, with Queenie naked and shaking so hard her breasts were jiggling, the man stripped her of her rings and the gold chain around her neck, though she was convinced by this time that the attack was surely no robbery – why undress her? – and was not for the purpose of rape either, though they might perform that evil act anyway.

These were Masters' men, and they were going to murder her.

Coco is on the bed, naked in Luk's arms, lying on top of her, slowly, sensuously rocking her hips, their pubes sliding against one another, stroking her forehead, kissing her, loving her, blissfully unaware of the terrifying drama unfolding next door. As her hips move backwards and forwards in tiny, orgiastic movements, her breasts dangle on Luk's, nipples brushing nipples, up down, up down, and Luk's fingers tightly grip Coco's buttocks, nails indenting the flesh, pulling and pushing along with Coco's little heaves.

Getting very close to climax, they cease all movement. Coco brushes a shiny black lock from Luk's eyes, and murmurs, 'Now?'

Luk grunts eager assent.

Moving her knees out from between Luk's, and to one side of her, Coco turns and straddles her body, lowering herself carefully until her crotch is above Luk's face. She buries her tongue in the crinkly-haired Chinese pussy as Luk's tongue finds her own.

In her armchair, Queenie was shaking measurably less as she fought for control, to be able to think, as the men's eyes never left her nakedness, lusting over it, though they made no move to sexually molest her. They were leaning on either side of the door, waiting for something, staring at her as if they were trying to leave the imprint of her nude body on their minds for ever.

There was an almost imperceptible knock on the door. The little man opened it, and Masters and Li slipped in. The door was closed with the tiniest click.

Two more pairs of eyes joined in the ogling. Queenie's flesh crawled, shrinking back from them. Masters grinned evilly at her, then pulled out a gun and moved to the stateroom door. Still nobody said a word.

Coco gasped her orgasm into Luk's pussy, as Luk sighed into hers. Her head rolled sideways into the girl's fleshy upper thigh and she closed her eyes. Seconds later, the door crashed open. Masters, menacing with his gun, filled the frame, Li squinting over his shoulder. In total shock, Coco peeked over Luk's thigh.

'Nice was it?' hissed Masters, baring his teeth. 'It 'appens to be my favourite fanny at the momen', 'n all. You, er, you won' be chuckin' me abou', this time.'

Li, also waving a gun, pushed past him, and Masters went back through the door. In front of Queenie, he stopped, ran a hand up the inside of her thigh, through her pubic bush and up over a breast, where it lingered, pinching. 'Pity to waste it, ain't it?' he sneered. 'Either of you two coolies fancy a screw, do it. Be quick abou' it and then ...' He nodded at the porthole. '... you know.'

He went back into the stateroom where Luk had rolled out from under Coco and was sitting on the bed with her feet on the deck. 'Sorry, doll,' she said, a look of genuine regret on her face. 'That was cool.' She nodded at Masters. 'But this is life, y'know?'

Coco seemed to be trying to melt into the safety of the mattress, cowering, her face contorted with fear.

Masters spat at the carpet. 'Prying little git!' he exclaimed. 'Told you I was gonna kill you!' He reached for a porthole and unlatched it. It was half a metre across, easily big enough to accommodate Coco's body. 'Two of the tastiest bits of meat those sharks 'ave ever 'ad, you lot!'

Paralysed with terror, Coco made no move as Masters ripped off her beaded necklace, then her watch. 'You wanna fuck 'er before I off 'er?' he asked Li.

'Better we finish with it quick,' said the Chinaman. He called out something in Chinese and the blue-suited man, who had been in the act of unzipping his trousers, appeared with his sticky tape. He wrapped it around Coco's legs, pinned her arms to her sides with it, and gagged her. Then he went back to Queenie, completed the job of unzipping himself, dropped on his knees in front of her and shoved her feet up on to his shoulders.

Masters and Li dropped their guns on the bed, picked up the thoroughly trussed Coco between them and began to shove her, feet first, through the open porthole. She struggled wildly and screamed into the sticky tape in vain.

With the big Chinaman about to penetrate Queenie, his sidekick leering, and Coco a third of the way out of the porthole, making the job of despatching her as difficult as possible with her struggling, all four of the men's attention was fully occupied.

There was a sudden, splintering crash as the cabin door was smashed in. Jamie, Dominic and Bobo spilled through it. Jamie and Dominic had guns, Bobo was wielding a big spanner.

Master's men were frozen with surprise long enough for them to constitute no problem. Bobo's spanner cracked into the side of the would-be rapist's skull and he toppled over, blood welling from a huge gash. The smaller man shrank away from Dominic's gun, his hands held over his head. Jamie, charging into the stateroom, let loose a single shot into the mattress, to convince Masters and Li to pull Coco back from the brink of death.

Then Helga also arrived with two pairs of handcuffs which she often put to rather more risqué use.

# 11

# More to Come?

. . . So, my friends, that is more or less the end of the story. Ah, I hear you say, a miraculously timely rescue, most convenient – but how was it possible? Simple. Helga, you see, was far more worried about the fate of Queenie and Coco at the hands of the villains than she cared to admit. They were an immensely evil, murderous bunch, and a massive amount of money was at stake. Convinced there would be an attempt on their lives, Helga did not want to frighten our heroes half to death. Whilst they were sight-seeing on the island of Marinduque, she had their suite bugged, the transmitter linked with a small speaker on the bridge, where it could be monitored twenty-four hours a day. This led to some extremely interesting listening for the helmsman on the night before the afternoon of the attack, when Queenie and Coco had made boisterous love – and it also saved their lives.

Jamie, of course, was in on the bugging and he put Dominic and Bobo in the picture. They were all ready to move fast at the slightest intimation of trouble.

The undercover, lesbian policewoman, who incidentally was not working alone, had managed to track down the final cocaine connection in Legaspi City, and in case she needed any more evidence to put Masters and Li away for a very long time, she also had them on charges of attempted murder at sea.

Queenie and Coco – well, they produced a fine article about the *Star of Kowloon* and her gamblers, which you can read in *Madame*, but I reckon, comparing them both, that my story is the rather more interesting. What do you think?

Francesca Jones, you mutter, is nothing but an outrageous sex maniac. Sex seems to be the activity which takes up at least half of her books. Guilty, I plead, and you had better do the same, had you not? After all, you have just read this story from cover to cover. Turn you on here and there, did it?

F.

## Letter from Esme

## Dear Readers

Here I am again, to tell you about the books that
Nexus have published in this verdant and vernal month
of May.

And I've made sure the publisher's chosen a
respectably clothed picture this month. I can't imagine
where he found the naughty photo he sneaked in at the
top of my letter last month.

*War in High Heels* is a sequel to *Spies in Silk*, in
which a brave band of young women received rigorous
training in the skills they needed to work behind enemy
lines in Nazi-occupied Europe. In the new book the girls
put their unusual techniques to work, seducing

Wehrmacht officers and liaising (that's a novel way of putting it!) with resistance fighters. Needless to say some of them are captured and subjected to all sorts of humiliating and painful ordeals at the hands of nasty Gestapo types. But with characteristic pluck, they win through at the climax.

*Queenie & Co* is the first book in a new series of three. That's Co without a full stop, because it's the name of Queenie's sidekick. Queenie is a ravishingly red-haired reporter, and Co is her oriental photographer. They are the best of friends and share absolutely everything! Their assignments takes them all over the world — Hong Kong, mainly, in this story — but they never seem to have much time to file copy or take photographs, because they have a habit of getting into situations where they just have to take all their clothes off and engage in vigorous bouts of sexual gymnastics. They don't seem to get tired, either.

The classic reprint is *Blue Angel Nights*, the first book in the trilogy about Weimar Germany and Hollywood between the wars by Margarete von Falkensee. Decadence and depravity, in sum.

Now, let me see. What's coming along next month? There's a bookful of forbidden treats in store for lovers of the Chronicles of Lidir: that most reclusive of authors, Aran Ashe, has been persuaded to pen another novel. Not a series this time, and not about Anya the slave princess — this is the tragic story of Justine, a young woman fated to experience love only in conjunction with shame, sadness and exquisite punishments. If you thought that the Lidir novels had exhausted all the possible combinations of restraint, chastisement and pleasure — think again.

Oh yes: the book's called *Choosing Lovers for Justine*.

Queenie and Coco, apparently still insatiable despite their remarkable exertions, will be at it again in *Queenie & Co in Japan*.

And the classic reprint will be *Blue Angel Secrets*, the third and last of the Blue Angel books. (The middle book, *Blue Angel Days*, was published in a new edition in 1992.)

And now, the really exciting news. I've been bursting to tell you about this for months, but the publisher wouldn't let me. Last time I visited his office I was determined to get my own way, though. You'd hardly believe what I can achieve in just five minutes with a short skirt, no knickers, and a chair wedged under the door handle. He soon came round to my point of view. Of course, I had to promise to do some pretty despicable things in return for being allowed to reveal the Big Secret.

Luckily, I like doing despicable things.

And the Big Secret is this: sex books for women, by the publishers of Nexus.

And about time too, I say. You men have been getting all the fun for far too long. We women can write just as well as you can (better, actually), and we like nothing better than getting really relaxed and cosy with a book that's hot and steamy.

Anyway, the books are going to be published under an imprint called Black Lace, and I expect you'll be hearing quite a lot about Black Lace books in the near future.

The first ones will go on sale in July 1993. And I can't wait to get my hands on them.

I'll tell you more just as soon as I've coaxed and cajoled more information from the publisher.

*Esmé*

# THE BEST IN EROTIC READING – BY POST·

The Nexus Library of Erotica – almost one hundred and fifty
volumes – is available from many booksellers and newsagents. If
you have any difficulty obtaining the books you require, you can
order them by post. Photocopy the list below, or tear the list out of
the book; then tick the titles you want and fill in the form at the end
of the list. Titles marked 1993 are not yet available: please do not try
to order them – just look out for them in the shops!

## CONTEMPORARY EROTICA

| | | | |
|---|---|---|---|
| AMAZONS | Erin Caine | £3.99 | |
| COCKTAILS | Stanley Carten | £3.99 | |
| CITY OF ONE-NIGHT STANDS | Stanley Carten | £4.50 | |
| CONTOURS OF DARKNESS | Marco Vassi | £4.99 | |
| THE GENTLE DEGENERATES | Marco Vassi | £4.99 | |
| MIND BLOWER | Marco Vassi | £4.99 | |
| THE SALINE SOLUTION | Marco Vassi | £4.99 | |
| DARK FANTASIES | Nigel Anthony | £4.99 | |
| THE DAYS AND NIGHTS OF MIGUMI | P.M. | £4.50 | |
| THE LATIN LOVER | P.M. | £3.99 | |
| THE DEVIL'S ADVOCATE | Anonymous | £4.50 | |
| DIPLOMATIC SECRETS | Antoine Lelouche | £3.50 | |
| DIPLOMATIC PLEASURES | Antoine Lelouche | £3.50 | |
| DIPLOMATIC DIVERSIONS | Antoine Lelouche | £4.50 | |
| ENGINE OF DESIRE | Alexis Arven | £3.99 | |
| DIRTY WORK | Alexis Arven | £3.99 | |
| DREAMS OF FAIR WOMEN | Celeste Arden | £2.99 | |
| THE FANTASY HUNTERS | Celeste Arden | £3.99 | |
| A GALLERY OF NUDES | Anthony Grey | £3.99 | |
| THE GIRL FROM PAGE 3 | Mike Angelo | £3.99 | |
| HELEN – A MODERN ODALISQUE | James Stern | £4.99 | 1993 |
| HOT HOLLYWOOD NIGHTS | Nigel Anthony | £4.50 | |
| THE INSTITUTE | Maria del Ray | £4.99 | |

| Title | Author | Price | Year |
|---|---|---|---|
| LAURE-ANNE | Laure-Anne | £4.50 | |
| LAURE-ANNE ENCORE | Laure-Anne | £4.99 | |
| LAURE-ANNE TOUJOURS | Laure-Anne | £4.99 | |
| Ms DEEDES ON A MISSION | Carole Andrews | £4.99 | 1993 |
| Ms DEEDES AT HOME | Carole Andrews | £4.50 | |
| Ms DEEDES ON PARADISE ISLAND | Carole Andrews | £4.99 | 1993 |
| MY SEX AND SOUL | Amelia Greene | £2.99 | |
| OBSESSION | Maria del Rey | £4.99 | 1993 |
| ONE WEEK IN THE PRIVATE HOUSE | Esme Ombreux | £4.50 | |
| PALACE OF FANTASIES | Delver Maddingley | £4.99 | |
| PALACE OF SWEETHEARTS | Delver Maddingley | £4.99 | |
| PALACE OF HONEYMOONS | Delver Maddingley | £4.99 | 1993 |
| PARADISE BAY | Maria del Rey | £4.50 | |
| QUEENIE AND CO | Francesca Jones | £4.99 | 1993 |
| QUEENIE AND CO IN JAPAN | Francesca Jones | £4.99 | 1993 |
| QUEENIE AND CO IN ARGENTINA | Francesca Jones | £4.99 | 1993 |
| THE SECRET WEB | Jane-Anne Roberts | £3.99 | |
| SECRETS LIE ON PILLOWS | James Arbroath | £4.50 | |
| SECRETS TIED IN SILK | James Arbroath | £4.99 | 1993 |
| STEPHANIE | Susanna Hughes | £4.50 | |
| STEPHANIE'S CASTLE | Susanna Hughes | £4.50 | |
| STEPHANIE'S DOMAIN | Susanna Hughes | £4.99 | 1993 |
| STEPHANIE'S REVENGE | Susanna Hughes | £4.99 | 1993 |
| THE DOMINO TATTOO | Cyrian Amberlake | £4.50 | |
| THE DOMINO ENIGMA | Cyrian Amberlake | £3.99 | |
| THE DOMINO QUEEN | Cyrian Amberlake | £4.99 | |

## EROTIC SCIENCE FICTION

|  |  |  | |
|---|---|---|---|
| ADVENTURES IN THE PLEASURE ZONE | Delaney Silver | £4.99 | |
| EROGINA | Christopher Denham | £4.50 | |
| HARD DRIVE | Stanley Carten | £4.99 | |
| PLEASUREHOUSE 13 | Agnetha Anders | £3.99 | |
| LAST DAYS OF THE PLEASUREHOUSE | Agnetha Anders | £4.50 | |
| TO PARADISE AND BACK | D.H.Master | £4.50 | |
| WICKED | Andrea Arven | £3.99 | |
| WILD | Andrea Arven | £4.50 | |

## ANCIENT & FANTASY SETTINGS

|  |  |  | |
|---|---|---|---|
| CHAMPIONS OF LOVE | Anonymous | £3.99 | |
| CHAMPIONS OF DESIRE | Anonymous | £3.99 | |

| | | | |
|---|---|---|---|
| CHAMPIONS OF PLEASURE | Anonymous | £3.50 | |
| THE SLAVE OF LIDIR | Aran Ashe | £4.50 | |
| DUNGEONS OF LIDIR | Aran Ashe | £4.99 | |
| THE FOREST OF BONDAGE | Aran Ashe | £4.50 | |
| KNIGHTS OF PLEASURE | Erin Caine | £4.50 | |
| PLEASURE ISLAND | Aran Ashe | £4.99 | |
| ROMAN ORGY | Marcus van Heller | £4.50 | |

## EDWARDIAN, VICTORIAN & OLDER EROTICA

| | | | |
|---|---|---|---|
| ADVENTURES OF A SCHOOLBOY | Anonymous | £3.99 | |
| THE AUTOBIOGRAPHY OF A FLEA | Anonymous | £2.99 | |
| BEATRICE | Anonymous | £3.99 | |
| THE BOUDOIR | Anonymous | £3.99 | |
| CASTLE AMOR | Erin Caine | £4.99 | 1993 |
| CHOOSING LOVERS FOR JUSTINE | Aran Ashe | £4.99 | 1993 |
| THE DIARY OF A CHAMBERMAID | Mirabeau | £2.99 | |
| THE LIFTED CURTAIN | Mirabeau | £4.99 | |
| EVELINE | Anonymous | £2.99 | |
| MORE EVELINE | Anonymous | £3.99 | |
| FESTIVAL OF VENUS | Anonymous | £4.50 | |
| 'FRANK' & I | Anonymous | £2.99 | |
| GARDENS OF DESIRE | Roger Rougiere | £4.50 | |
| OH, WICKED COUNTRY | Anonymous | £2.99 | |
| LASCIVIOUS SCENES | Anonymous | £4.50 | |
| THE LASCIVIOUS MONK | Anonymous | £4.50 | |
| LAURA MIDDLETON | Anonymous | £3.99 | |
| A MAN WITH A MAID 1 | Anonymous | £4.99 | |
| A MAN WITH A MAID 2 | Anonymous | £4.99 | |
| A MAN WITH A MAID 3 | Anonymous | £4.99 | |
| MAUDIE | Anonymous | £2.99 | |
| THE MEMOIRS OF DOLLY MORTON | Anonymous | £4.50 | |
| A NIGHT IN A MOORISH HAREM | Anonymous | £3.99 | |
| PARISIAN FROLICS | Anonymous | £2.99 | |
| PLEASURE BOUND | Anonymous | £3.99 | |
| THE PLEASURES OF LOLOTTE | Andrea de Nerciat | £3.99 | |
| THE PRIMA DONNA | Anonymous | £3.99 | |
| RANDIANA | Anonymous | £4.50 | |
| REGINE | E.K. | £2.99 | |

| | | |
|---|---|---|
| THE ROMANCE OF LUST 1 | Anonymous | £3.99 |
| THE ROMANCE OF LUST 2 | Anonymous | £2.99 |
| ROSA FIELDING | Anonymous | £2.99 |
| SUBURBAN SOULS 1 | Anonymous | £2.99 |
| SURBURBAN SOULS 2 | Anonymous | £3.99 |
| THREE TIMES A WOMAN | Anonymous | £2.99 |
| THE TWO SISTERS | Anonymous | £3.99 |
| VIOLETTE | Anonymous | £4.99 |

## "THE JAZZ AGE"

| | | |
|---|---|---|
| ALTAR OF VENUS | Anonymous | £3.99 |
| THE SECRET GARDEN ROOM | Georgette de la Tour | £3.50 |
| BEHIND THE BEADED CURTAIN | Georgette de la Tour | £3.50 |
| BLANCHE | Anonymous | £3.99 |
| BLUE ANGEL NIGHTS | Margaret von Falkensee | £4.99 |
| BLUE ANGEL DAYS | Margaret von Falkensee | £4.99 |
| BLUE ANGEL SECRETS | Margaret von Falkensee | £4.99 |
| CAROUSEL | Anonymous | £4.50 |
| CONFESSIONS OF AN ENGLISH MAID | Anonymous | £3.99 |
| FLOSSIE | Anonymous | £2.50 |
| SABINE | Anonymous | £3.99 |
| PLAISIR D'AMOUR | Anne-Marie Villefranche | £4.50 |
| FOLIES D'AMOUR | Anne-Marie Villefranche | £2.99 |
| JOIE D'AMOUR | Anne-Marie Villefranche | £3.99 |
| MYSTERE D'AMOUR | Anne-Marie Villefranche | £3.99 |
| SECRETS D'AMOUR | Anne-Marie Villefranche | £3.50 |
| SOUVENIR D'AMOUR | Anne-Marie Villefranche | £3.99 |

## WORLD WAR 2

| | | | |
|---|---|---|---|
| SPIES IN SILK | Piers Falconer | £4.50 | |
| WAR IN HIGH HEELS | Piers Falconer | £4.99 | 1993 |

## CONTEMPORARY FRENCH EROTICA (translated into English)

| | | |
|---|---|---|
| EXPLOITS OF A YOUNG DON JUAN | Anonymous | £2.99 |
| INDISCREET MEMOIRS | Alain Dorval | £2.99 |
| INSTRUMENT OF PLEASURE | Celeste Piano | £4.50 |
| JOY | Joy Laurey | £2.99 |
| JOY AND JOAN | Joy Laurey | £2.99 |

| | | |
|---|---|---|
| JOY IN LOVE | Joy Laurey | £2.75 |
| LILIANE | Paul Verguin | £3.50 |
| MANDOLINE | Anonymous | £3.99 |
| LUST IN PARIS | Antoine S. | £4.99 |
| NYMPH IN PARIS | Galia S. | £2.99 |
| SCARLET NIGHTS | Juan Muntaner | £3.99 |
| SENSUAL LIAISONS | Anonymous | £3.50 |
| SENSUAL SECRETS | Anonymous | £3.99 |
| THE NEW STORY OF O | Anonymous | £4.50 |
| THE IMAGE | Jean de Berg | £3.99 |
| VIRGINIE | Nathalie Perreau | £4.50 |
| THE PAPER WOMAN | Francois Rey | £4.50 |

## SAMPLERS & COLLECTIONS

| | | |
|---|---|---|
| EROTICON 1 | ed. J-P Spencer | £4.50 |
| EROTICON 2 | ed. J-P Spencer | £4.50 |
| EROTICON 3 | ed. J-P Spencer | £4.50 |
| EROTICON 4 | ed. J-P Spencer | £4.99 |
| NEW EROTICA 1 | ed. Esme Ombreux | £4.99 |
| THE FIESTA LETTERS | ed. Chris Lloyd | £4.50 |
| THE PLEASURES OF LOVING | ed. Maren Sell | £3.99 |

## NON-FICTION

| | | | |
|---|---|---|---|
| HOW TO DRIVE YOUR MAN WILD IN BED | Graham Masterton | £4.50 | |
| HOW TO DRIVE YOUR WOMAN WILD IN BED | Graham Masterton | £3.99 | |
| HOW TO BE THE PERFECT LOVER | Graham Masterton | £2.99 | |
| FEMALE SEXUAL AWARENESS | Barry & Emily McCarthy | £5.99 | |
| LINZI DREW'S PLEASURE GUIDE | Linzi Drew | £4.99 | |
| LETTERS TO LINZI | Linzi Drew | £4.99 | 1993 |
| WHAT MEN WANT | Susan Crain Bakos | £3.99 | |
| YOUR SEXUAL SECRETS | Marty Klein | £3.99 | |

---

Please send me the books I have ticked above.

Name ...............................................

Address ...............................................

...............................................

........................Post code .............

Send to: **Nexus Books Cash Sales, PO Box 11, Falmouth, Cornwall, TR10 9EN**

Please enclose a cheque or postal order, made payable to **Nexus Books**, to the value of the books you have ordered plus postage and packing costs as follows:

UK and BFPO – £1.00 for the first book, 50p for the second book, and 30p for each subsequent book to a maximum of £3.00;

Overseas (including Republic of Ireland) – £2.00 for the first book, £1.00 for the second book, and 50p for each subsequent book.

If you would prefer to pay by VISA or ACCESS/MASTERCARD, please write your card number here:

— — — —    — — — —    — — — —    — — — —

**Signature:** _____